THE HOUSE IN ABERCROMBY SQUARE
and
MISTRESS OF LUKE'S FOLLY

Elizabeth Elgin is the bestselling author of *All the Sweet Promises, Whisper on the Wind, I'll Bring You Buttercups* and *Daisychain Summer.* She served in the WRNS during the Second World War and met her husband on board a submarine depot ship. A keen gardener, she has two daughters and five grandsons and lives in a village in the Vale of York.

D1323756

ELIZABETH ELGIN

The House in Abercromby Square

Mistress of Luke's Folly

Grafton

HarperCollins*Publishers*
77-85 Fulham Palace Road,
Hammersmith, London W6 8JB

This one-volume paperback edition 1995

Reprinted in 2003

The House in Abercromby Square first published
by Robert Hale & Company 1976
Mistress of Luke's Folly first published
by Robert Hale & Company 1981

Copyright © Elizabeth Elgin 1976, 1981 and 1995

Elizabeth Elgin asserts the moral right to
be identified as the author of these works

ISBN 0 00 768307 3

Set in Linotron Sabon
at The Spartan Press Ltd,
Lymington, Hants

Printed and bound in Great Britain by
Mackays of Chatham Ltd, Chatham, Kent

Contents

The House in
Abercromby Square

One

'But Patrick, *dearest* Patrick,' Arabella Harrington's small pale forefinger intimately traced the hairline of the man in whose arms she stood, 'why must you go to Liverpool? It is a nasty, dirty place — you have said so yourself. Why must you get a sudden urge to visit your aunt and completely upset Papa's holiday arrangements?'

'Because, my love,' Patrick Norris sighed, 'there are things I must do before we are married and,' he added almost as an afterthought, 'I have not seen Aunt Hetty for nearly three years.'

'But why *now*?' The soft mouth arranged itself into a childish pout. 'Since I have known you, you have scarcely mentioned your family in Liverpool and now, when we are all ready to travel to Harrogate, you announce you are going elsewhere. Papa is not a little put out!'

Patrick smiled into the small face upturned to his. Even now, he could hardly believe his good fortune in being accepted as Robert Harrington's future son-in-law. He had no wish to upset the wealthy Harley Street physician who employed him, nor for that matter, to cause one moment of annoyance to Arabella.

Gently he kissed the tip of her pert, dainty nose. She had, he thought, with her white skin and eyes blue as periwinkles, the fragility of a china shepherdess and when she tilted her head, her pale yellow ringlets bobbed about her ears in a way he found endearingly irresistible.

'I am sorry, Bella, if I have upset your plans but it is important that I visit my aunt. I will join you in Harrogate within three days at the most – surely you will not die of a broken heart in so short a time?' he teased.

'I will try not to, Patrick.'

She gave him a small smile, 'Though I will miss you on the journey. I had looked forward to your company. I have never travelled by railroad before. It would have been comforting to have you with me.'

'But you will have your father to take care of you, dearest, and the railroads are safe as houses.'

'I know, but . . .'

Arabella released herself from his arms, whisking her frilled muslin skirts to show a flurry of lace petticoat and a disturbing glimpse of pretty ankle. She stood by the broad window, her back to him, ' . . . but since we are to be married, I would have thought that my wishes came before all else.'

'They do, my love, and they always will, you know that. It is merely that my aunt must be told about our marriage. It is common courtesy – surely you will allow me that?'

'But you have already written to her about it and she did not allow *us* the courtesy of a reply!' came back the tart retort.

Patrick sighed. Motherless since babyhood, Arabella, the only child of a doting father, had been outrageously spoiled and though blessed with a usually sunny nature, there were times when she could be wilful as a small child when her wishes were flouted. When they were married thought Patrick with a flush of unease, he must take a firm hand with Bella's little moods.

It seemed strange that he found it impossible to confess to the woman who was to be his wife that Aunt Hetty had not sent her blessing because, quite simply, Aunt Hetty had never learned to read or write.

He felt a small prick of annoyance that he could not confide the fact to Arabella. Aunt Hester Norris had been mother and father to him. He loved her dearly and he would admit her shortcomings to no one. Nor could he bring himself to admit to Arabella that there were things he now felt he should be told; things about himself and his past.

Many times before, when he was a young medical apprentice, he had tried to broach the matter but Aunt Hetty, with her usual adroitness had sidestepped his efforts. Now, with his marriage to Arabella Harrington soon to take place, Patrick felt the time had come to take a firm stand. The *Private Matter* must be brought into the open. And besides, he reasoned, if things were as he supposed it would be all to his advantage in this new society to which he would soon belong; a society into which, if he were truthful, he had tenaciously fought to enter.

Patrick had small vague memories of his past but they amounted to nothing more than fleeting remembrances of large, lofty rooms; of an elegant staircase and rows of bells on circular, bobbing springs.

But one thing was certain in his mind. Not all Arabella's pouting or pleading and, most probably, even her pretty tears, would prevent him from visiting Aunt Hetty at Liverpool.

And there was Adam, too. Suddenly Patrick had felt a longing to see his friend and talk over old times with him. He wanted to know how Adam was making out in the life he had chosen and exactly what Adam's last letter had meant to imply.

Deliberately Patrick shut down his thoughts and walked towards Arabella's indignant little back. Gently he placed his arms around her tiny waist, pulling her close to him, whispering softly into her sweet-smelling hair.

'Darling Bella, we must not quarrel. Tell me how much you love me.'

But Miss Arabella Harrington was now firmly astride her high-horse and deftly removed his hands.

'Patrick, you must not hold me so intimately when we are alone,' she chided. 'It is not seemly and besides, one of the servants might come in.'

Patrick cupped the indignant face in his hands.

'I don't care about the servants.'

'Well I do!' Angrily she brushed past him, 'and so should *you*, Patrick!'

There were bright spots of colour now in her soft cheeks and her blue eyes flashed dangerously. Soon, thought Patrick, there will be tears and that he must avoid at all costs. Bella was being unreasonable but he cared for her and he did not like to see her cry, not even when her tears were slightly suspect.

'Arabella, my dear, if you command me not to go to Liverpool then I shall not go. But can you, sweet creature that you are, deny two days of my company to an old lady who has not seen me in years? Can you do this?' he rushed on as an uncertain sniff told him she was weakening, 'when soon you will have me all to yourself for the rest of our lives?'

He paused, his eyes pleading, hoping his cajoling had made its mark. Then suddenly she was in his arms telling him she was being selfish and that it was only because she loved him so dearly that she hated to be parted from him.

'Forgive your Bella,' she pleaded, so earnestly that he promptly kissed her, partly from affection and partly from relief.

'Come, darling,' he coaxed. 'It is a lovely evening. Get your bonnet and cape and we will take a turn in the park. Remember, I will be leaving very early in the morning. Let us hold hands where there are no servants to interrupt us and I will tell you again how dear you are to me.'

Eagerly she agreed, for as much as she was able, Arabella loved him.

Patrick stood by the ornate glass panel of the booking-office and took two sovereigns from his purse.

'A single fare to Liverpool — first class.'

'Change at Manchester, sir.'

Respectfully the ticket clerk nodded his head.

Despite the early hour, Euston Square station was busy and noisy. It would not be long, thought Patrick, before the railroads had quite outstripped road travel. A journey by steam-train was more comfortable and reliable than by coach-and-four and it was quicker by far with no overnight stops at inns or hostels. Why, he reasoned, given a good driver they would be in Liverpool by night-fall.

A small hunchbacked porter picked up his bags.

'The Manchester train, sir?'

The man, Patrick realized with not a little pleasure, had taken it for granted that his services would be required. But then, he was fast becoming aware of the fact that a gentleman must never carry his own baggage. And not only in his new prosperity was Patrick beginning to dress like a gentleman, he was also becoming to feel like one. In his checked trousers, his topcoat with its matching checked edging, a fine tall hat and hand-sewn gloves, he was well satisfied that he looked the part.

He sniffed the smell of sulphur and grease that mingled with coal-smoke and listened to the hiss of escaping steam, a faint excitement stirring inside him. He still felt a sense of adventure when he entered a railway station. He could understand Arabella's apprehension at the thought of such a journey. Soon she and her father would be leaving for Harrogate but since Doctor Harrington was of the opinion that to travel such a distance would be too much for Arabella's constitution, he had decided to stay overnight in Leeds and make the remainder of the journey by coach. The drive over the moors to Harrogate in the clear air he considered, would be extremely beneficial, provided they were well wrapped up.

Patrick indicated the centre door of the three-compartment gentlemen's carriage. The London and North-Western Railway Company looked well after their passengers, he thought. The seats were soft and well-sprung and the floor was covered with fine quality carpeting. At the windows, plush curtains ensured privacy should the traveller wish it.

He watched as his bags and tall tin hat-box were placed on the seat beside him, then, handing the man a penny, he pulled up the window as a precaution against smoke and smuts and a possible invasion of fellow-travellers.

By mid-day, Patrick had tired of watching people and houses and fields slipping past the windows. At first, the sight of green fields and cow-pastures and thickly-wooded slopes had filled him with pleasure. It was so different, he thought, from the crowded, roistering town he was travelling towards at a steady thirty miles each hour. Liverpool was, as the dour-faced Doctor Duncan had so often stressed, the dirtiest, most unhealthy town in the whole of Europe. And Doctor Duncan, whose lectures he and Adam had attended at the Medical Institution in their student days, was an authority on dirt. It had seemed to the young pupils that the worthy Scotsman was obsessed by the squalor of Liverpool's meaner streets, of the airless courts of small houses and the need for a decent supply of fresh water and properly laid sewers. They had joked about his preoccupation with and perpetual grumbling about the matter but they had known, inexperienced as they were, that every word he preached was nothing short of the truth.

Patrick sighed and opened his hat-box. It was packed with food, socks, clean handkerchiefs and the large, thick muffler Aunt Hetty once knitted. Soon, of course, he would be able to afford more than one top-hat but at the moment the tall black box with its patterns of gold-leaf scrolls was more a symbol of his new-found status than the receptacle for which it was intended.

Gratefully he unwound the white starched napkin from a half-bottle of wine and placed it across his knees. Doctor Harrington's cook, he decided as he unpacked the parcel of chicken legs, was the treasure of a woman for she had thoughtfully provided peaches and apples for his dessert. He was glad that after their marriage, he and Arabella would continue to live in the large house in Harley Street, assured still of every attention to their comfort.

He wondered what smell of cooking would greet his nostrils tonight when he opened the door of Aunt Hetty's little house. Would it be one of her famous stews, a stockpot of broth, or good, nourishing cow-heels? He had come a long way since his cow-heel days, Patrick thought with a downward quirk of his mouth. Now, he ate at Robert Harrington's elegant table, gracefully laid with crisp white linen, silver, and bowls of flowers. And no meal was considered acceptable unless it was accompanied by at least two wines. He had quickly adapted himself to such luxury but then, it had not been all that difficult a task. He had intended right from the start that it should be so. From the beginning of his apprenticeship, Patrick Norris knew exactly where he was going. Liverpool was of no use to him, he long ago decided. When his apprenticeship was over and his examinations taken, he vowed that no less a place than London should have the benefit of his undoubted talent and that nothing and no one should be allowed to stand in his unswerving path.

'But, Patrick,' Adam had protested, 'do you feel nothing for these poor people? Doesn't your conscience upset you when you talk of leaving Liverpool?'

'It does not!' Patrick had grimly retorted. 'I have slaved for five years, Adam, and come the day when I face the Board in London and pass my examiners, this town has seen the last of Patrick Norris, I promise you!'

'I cannot believe that you mean it,' Adam's gentle face showed concern. 'They are your people. Don't you owe them something? Don't you want to help them? Heaven knows,' Adam's blue eyes were troubled, 'they are not able to help themselves.'

Patrick had laughed.

'There is a saying that heaven aids him who aids himself. Well, Adam, I have been giving heaven a gentle shove for years, now!'

'Then I am sorry, Patrick.'

The soft voice held no anger.

'Why should *you* be sorry, Adam Carmichael? What

do you know of life save what you've seen in those stinking wards? You were born to position and wealth. You've never tipped your cap to your betters or had your backside kicked by them. What do you know?' he demanded, angrily. 'When have you ever tasted poverty?'

But Adam had only smiled.

'Perhaps, Patrick,' he said sadly, 'I would have been a better person if I had.'

Patrick shook away his thoughts and reached for a peach.

It had all been talk, he supposed. True, Adam Carmichael had stayed in Liverpool but his address was a good one. Abercromby Square in which he now lived was populated by merchants and shipowners. Its houses were tall and grand with well-kept gardens in the centre of the square. He remembered it from his childhood. Those who lived there owned their own carriages and many drove out with a footman in attendance.

Whatever Adam's intentions had been in their student days, he had certainly picked himself a good address from which to practise, Patrick decided.

Still, he thought as he lowered the window and threw out the remains of his luncheon and the empty wine bottle, it would be good to see Adam again. He remembered the pale, gentle face with its shock of fair curls tumbling about it as though it were only yesterday they had shaken hands and parted. For all that, he had been a little surprised when, not so long ago, he had read Adam's last letter.

There is so much work here, Patrick. I need you . . .

Patrick shrugged his shoulders. It was a pity, he thought, but *he* didn't need Adam. No matter how busy a practice Adam might have built up, it could not offer one small part, Patrick decided, of the benefits in store for him in London.

It all started, he supposed, the day he and Adam had taken the steam-train to London. They had completed their Liverpool apprenticeships; dutifully attended the lectures demanded of them; done more than their fair stint of work in infirmary wards and now all that remained was the final hurdle – the grand gentlemen of the Board of Examiners.

Luck had been with Patrick that day, for Arabella's father had been a member of that board made up of surgeons, apothecaries and physicians; one of the elite who sat in their solemnity and decided whether finally a student might be accepted as a licentiate of the Society of Apothecaries and call himself a doctor, at last. On that day, Doctor Robert Harrington, on the look-out for an assistant, invited Patrick to join his London practice.

And so he had come to Harley Street, that broad thoroughfare of grand houses and favoured by doctors, originally, because of its close proximity to the railway stations along the Euston Road that brought in patients from the provinces.

From that day on, he had taken to Harley Street as though he had been born to it and he had never looked back. Soon, on his marriage to his employer's only child, he would be made a partner. One day he would be a rich man and a man of property when Arabella came into her birthright.

Return to Liverpool? Return to those mean streets when he had spent half of his life getting away from them? Give up the promise of wealth because Adam needed him?

'Ha!'

He let out a small, derisive laugh.

Sorry, Adam, old friend, whispered his conscience, *it will be good to see you again, but . . .*

Besides, thought Patrick, it wasn't as though he was making this journey solely to talk over old times with Adam. Far from it. The reason for his visit was a firm intention to wrest from Aunt Hetty the truth of his parentage. It was plain that Hester Norris was in no way related to him other than perhaps by the ties of love they felt for each other. Patrick was, he was sure, of nobler birth than anything Aunt Hetty could have bestowed upon him. He had been certain of it for a very long time. Aunt Hetty was an ordinary working woman; she had no private means or any other income that he knew of. Some person of substance must, he was sure, have made her some allowance.

But his aunt could be tight-lipped as a stone statue when it suited her purpose and it suited her to become vague or forgetful whenever Patrick had tried to broach what he had come to regard as the *Private Matter*. Now, with his marriage into the upper-middle class imminent, the truth about the *Private Matter* must be made known to him. A man had the right to know about his parentage, if only for the sake of his wife and children.

Of course, being a love-child would not exactly be acceptable in the polite society that surrounded Doctor Harrington, but being the love-child, perhaps, of the daughter of a family of substance would be a little more decent. His mother – his *real* mother, that was – had been a lady born, he was sure of it and a lady of means into the bargain for who else could have paid for his education? It had been an expensive business he knew and utterly beyond the means of Aunt Hetty Norris.

Norris. It was the only name he had ever known but it couldn't be his real name. Would he perhaps, when the truth became known, take his mother's name? It might well be to his advantage, the more so if it were a well-known name. Patrick Johnstone, perhaps? One of the Liverpool Johnstones, the shipowners, don't you know?

Had Aunt Hetty been his nurse in that vaguely-remembered house with the sweeping staircase and the rooms so tall that they seemed to a small boy to reach right up to God?

Would his family, once they had been acquainted with the success he had become, be willing to acknowledge him as one of themselves? They must at least be a benevolent family for he could never remember being hungry or going barefoot as a small boy; he had never worked or sold matches in the streets; had never heard the rent-collector hammering on the door. His real family were good people at heart and what was more, he had good blood in his veins. Now he must be told whose it was. It mattered a great deal to him. Aunt Hetty must be silent no longer.

Irritably, Patrick stared out of the window. The green fields had given way now to scattered knots of houses; small, greystone dwellings so reminiscent of the north country. Soon the sprawling mills would dominate the landscape, their chimneys spewing foul black smoke, their shuttles clacking out prosperity for some fortunate owner. Soon, he would be in Manchester where the new machines had ousted the craftsmen spinners and weavers and brought more poverty to the poor and more riches to the rich. The mill-owners cared little that their money sprung from grass roots set in misery and muck.

But that was the order of things, reasoned Patrick now unashamedly attached to middle-class thinking.

He stretched his legs luxuriously. They had made good time to Manchester for it was still only late afternoon. Soon he would change trains for Liverpool. He was impatient, now, to be there, for the sooner he arrived, the sooner he could do what he had set out to do and then be gone.

The sun was setting, sinking it seemed into the summer-calm waters of the river Mersey when the train clanked and shuddered into the glass-domed vastness of Liverpool's Lime Street station. Almost at once, mingling with the railway smell, Patrick caught the stench of the closely-populated streets. It was so instantly familiar that for a moment he could scarcely believe he had ever left them. With a feeling that was almost distaste, he deposited his baggage at the luggage office. He intended to walk to Aunt Hetty's house for a horse and cab drawing up at the small cottage in Lace Street would attract too much attention, he decided. It was only a few minutes walk and he was not as yet so well-endowed that he could afford to waste what he had on unnecessary expenditure.

He crossed the road, resisting the cries of small ragged boys who touted for the cab drivers, closing his ears to the mongrel accent that was part Lancashire and part Welsh and Irish.

'Give us a ha'penny for a hot tattie, sir?'

Patrick looked down at the small pinched face of the dirty child who trotted beside him.

'Only a ha'penny for a hot supper, me lord?'

A ha'penny for a tattie, was it? Patrick knew full well that the ha'penny and all the other coins the street-waif begged would be handed over to a shiftless father and end up in the ale-house before nightfall. But he fished in his pocket for a small coin and threw it on the pavement.

'Be off with you!' he jerked, ashamed almost of his stupidity. Then he quickened his steps lest before long the word went round that there was an open-handed toff in the vicinity and he became surrounded by hordes of child-beggars.

He turned sharply from Fontenoy Street, trying not to see the choked gutters, the barefoot mothers and children and women who stood brazenly, offering their bodies for the price of a loaf of bread or a slug of gin. He was glad when he reached the little court at the end of Lace Street.

It shocked him that it looked even smaller and meaner than ever he remembered it. At one end the stand-tap that provided water for the little huddle of houses was surrounded by women, patiently waiting with jugs and buckets until it dripped and splashed into life for a brief half-hour before it was again turned off for the night. And at the other end of the court the stench of the open midden told him he was home again.

Had it always smelled so foul? he wondered. Had the gracious London street in which he now lived dimmed the memory of his early years? Only one thing had not changed and his heart lifted a little at the sight of Hetty Norris's small house as it stood out clean and shining amidst the squalor.

The door-stone was newly scoured and the uneven flags outside swilled clean. The windows sparkled brightly, softly illuminated by the light of a single candle.

Gently Patrick lifted the door-latch and stepped into the small bare room. No fire burned in the grate but from the back of the house came the familiar smell of the clothes-boiler and the pungent odour of primrose soap.

Dear Aunt Hetty. Patrick's heart throbbed with long-forgotten love. She was still doing her washing for charity, as she called it.

'Hullo?' he called in a voice that was rough with emotion.

Then she was standing there, her grey wispy hair hanging in damp strands about her face, her body looking smaller and frailer than he had ever remembered, with a look of such unspeakable joy in her tired eyes that for a moment Patrick felt a wave of shame he had never thought possible.

For a moment he stood still, his eyes taking in her fragility and the defiant tilt of her head. Then he stepped forward and gathered her into his arms, lifting her towards him, holding her close.

'Aunt Hetty,' he breathed.

Two

For a little while Patrick held her to him, surprised that she felt so light in his arms, so very fragile. It was, he thought, like lifting a small child.

'Dear Aunt Hetty,' he whispered. 'Oh, but it's been so long . . .'

'Impudent boy! Put me down this instant! Have you forgotten how a lady should be treated since you went away?'

But there was kindness in her eyes and love and laughter and Patrick felt her warm tears on his cheek as they held each other close.

'Let me look at you.'

She held him at arm's length and gazed into his face.

'My, but aren't you just the fine gentleman? Aren't you the handsome one?'

Her eyes took in his crinkly black hair, cut now in the fashionably longer London style; hair that had caused him many a fight in his childhood, she remembered fondly when local lads had yelled,

'*Curly! Curly! Hair like a girlie!*'

And his newly-grown black moustache – how it suited him. What a fine young man he had become. It had all been worth it, she thought proudly.

'You'll be hungry, boy,' she said in her usual practical way. 'Are you getting enough to eat? They do say that

London women haven't the same way with the cooking
as we have up here.'

Patrick thought of the skill of Robert Harrington's
cook and the remains of the plenteous luncheon he had
thrown from the carriage window.

'I do tolerably well, Aunt; tolerably well, thank you.'

'Then you shall sit down and have a meal and tell me
how long you plan to stay.'

She gave a small, excited laugh. 'Oh, we have so much
talking to do. There is so much I want to know.'

'But you got my letters, Aunt?'

'I did, boy. I did. And the Reverend read them all to
me. But you must tell me more about your little sweet-
heart, Patrick. Does she cook well, and mend and sew?'

Patrick thought about Arabella. It would be useless to
try to explain to Aunt Hetty that in fashionable London
society young ladies were expected to lead inactive lives;
to look pale and decorative and to faint at the dropping
of a lace-edged handkerchief.

Cook? He doubted if Arabella had ever filled a kettle of
water in the whole of her nineteen years.

'Miss Harrington will make me a good wife, Aunt,' he
returned gravely.

'And does she go regular to church and say her prayers
at night?'

'She does, Aunt.'

That at least was the truth.

Hetty Norris busied herself with laying the table. The
cloth was patched but snowy white and heavily starched.
She set out a knife and fork and mug and laid a plate of
brawn before him.

'And the Queen, Patrick? Have you seen dear Queen
Victoria?'

'Indeed I have. She is an extremely gracious lady. She

often rides in her carriage in the park near Harley Street. I have had the privilege of raising my hat as she drove past.'

'*Ahhhh!*'

For a moment, such news silenced even Miss Hetty's excited tongue.

Patrick looked with distaste at the homely pig's-head brawn but at least, he thought, it wasn't cow-heel!

Suddenly he wasn't hungry but he broke a piece of bread and on finding there was no butter on the table, started reluctantly to eat.

'Are you not joining me, Aunt Hetty?'

'No, Patrick. No, I'm not hungry and besides, when you get older you'll find a body needs less food inside it.'

Patrick sliced into the meat on his plate, letting it slip down his throat without tasting it.

Aunt Hetty pulled up a chair.

'I'll join you in a mug of tea, though,' she said, settling down to hear his news.

'I fear I shall not be able to stay, Aunt.'

Best he should make his point before the old woman had time to make up the bed in the little top room.

'Not stay, boy?'

Hetty Norris's face registered disbelief and disappointment.

'I am due in Harrogate to meet my employer in two days' time and I have promised to call on Adam Carmichael.'

'Ah, Adam.'

A look of tenderness crossed the tired face.

'He is a good man, Patrick. He has called to see me several times since you left. We talk about you a lot and about the old days.'

'Is he doing well?'

Patrick was glad that further protests about his too-early departure seemed to have been successfully side-tracked.

'Adam tells me very little about his practice in his letters.'

'He works very hard. People trust him. He is a good doctor and he is a gentleman, too.'

'He was *born* a gentleman,' Patrick retorted, roughly. Then, without raising his head from his plate he said, 'I have something to ask you, Aunt Hetty. I want you to give me a truthful answer.'

'Yes, boy?'

A guarded look crept into the faded blue eyes.

'What is my real name, Aunt? I think I should be told, now.'

He asked the question abruptly as if he hoped the sudden approach would find the old woman unprepared, but she raised her head and looked him steadily in the eyes.

'It is Patrick Norris,' she said, evenly, 'the name you have had for twenty-six years. If there is another, it slips my memory, for the moment.'

'*If* there is another? There must be another, unless I am *your* son!'

He flushed guiltily. He had not meant to be so direct.

'That was a foolish thing to say, Patrick,' was the only reply she gave.

'I am sorry, Aunt, but with my marriage approaching I feel I should be told more about myself. I have a right to know.'

'No man has a right to *anything*, boy. You are Patrick Norris and you have been loved and wanted since I first set eyes on you. That is all you need to know. Some day, perhaps . . .'

The voice trailed off into a weary silence and Patrick knew he had been thwarted again. But this time he was determined he would not give in so easily.

'It is likely I will stay the night at Adam's house,' he replied, 'but I will see you before I leave.'

He lifted her hand and held it to his cheek.

'Aunt Hetty, won't you tell me?'

He made one last despairing appeal.

'I will see you tomorrow,' she said quietly and sadly as she walked ahead of him to the door.

Slowly the horse strained up the steep incline of the street most ineptly named Mount Pleasant, weariness echoing in each hollow step. Like himself, thought Patrick, the horse and driver had probably been up since early dawn. It would be pleasant to be received warmly into the comfort of Adam's home. He was surprised that he should feel so dispirited and spent.

'Which number, sir?' called the cab driver.

'Thirteen, if you please.'

'That'll be Doctor Adam's place. Folks around these parts call it *The Haven*.'

Patrick did not reply. He was not now in the habit of engaging in conversations with cab drivers unless it suited his purpose. But it suited him quickly enough as they turned slowly into Abercromby Square.

'What on earth . . .?' he jerked.

Gone was the air of prosperous respectability. Many of the houses appeared to be empty or badly neglected and a great many more seemed to be bulging with a surfeit of occupants.

'Well might you remark, sir. Bit of a mess, ain't it? But they can get ten or a dozen into one of them big rooms. It's pretty plain you've not visited these parts for some time.'

The sight of the once-proud houses shocked Patrick into silence.

'It's the in-comers you see, squire. Landing by the boatload, poor creatures.'

Patrick knew about the Irish immigrants, forced from their own country by the hunger that followed the repeated failure of their potato crops; knew too that Liverpool was the first step in their bid to reach the promised land that was America and the new life and new freedom they hoped to find there.

'But they don't live *here*, in Abercromby Square?'

'Not so's you'd notice, sir, but they're crowding out the lodging-houses and even bedding down in old ware-houses. Local folks is getting out and since the gentlemen from these fine houses have taken themselves off, it's natural that others should move in.'

He shrugged.

'It's bad for trade, an' all. The gentry have moved out, up to Everton Heights and West Derby and such-like better places. Can't blame 'em, either, only it's a pity . . .'

He shook his head like a mournful old dog.

'But why?'

The lodging-houses and tenements and warehouses were to be found along the waterfront, Patrick reasoned. Surely they need not have concerned those people who had lived in comparative isolation in Abercromby Square?

'Well, sir, there's the water shortage for one thing. Not enough to go round now, with all the extra folks come in from Ireland and there's the troubles they brings with 'em!'

'Troubles?'

'Aye,' the man nodded his head sagely. 'Like the thieving and the street-women. They've got no money and stands to reason they got to eat. And there's the fevers and Lord-knows what else. They do say as there's more cholera by the tobacco warehouses. I has to be very careful who I picks up, these days!'

Patrick wanted to hear no more. Quite suddenly he wanted to place the distance of many miles between himself and Liverpool.

Without a thought he handed a florin to the driver and only vaguely heard the surprised, 'Coo! God bless yer, squire!' as he slowly walked up the steps of the house that was numbered thirteen.

Its door was thrown wide open. Beside it a highly-polished brass plate bore the name *Adam Carmichael L.S.A.*

Patrick's feet echoed loudly on the uncovered, spotlessly-clean floor, vibrating to the ornately moulded ceiling that had obviously not felt the ministrations of a decorator's brush in years.

On the walls, faded red silk covering reminded of an earlier prosperity and an elegant, uncarpeted staircase curved upwards to a large bare window on the half-landing.

Patrick blinked his eyes with disbelief. What would he think now, that man who once must have lived here in splendour if he were suddenly to return? What could have happened? Patrick demanded silently of himself. The comfort he had imagined to find in the home of a man who lived in Abercromby Square was nowhere to be seen. That some kind of surgery was in progress was obvious he decided, glancing at the huddle of miserably-dressed people who sat without a murmur of complaint in the bare lofty hall.

Bemused, he sat down to wait at the end of one of the well-scrubbed benches. Glancing at the quietly-waiting patients his professional eye quickly diagnosed a goitre, a well-pregnant woman suffering from malnutrition, two cases of rickets, a woman who obviously had contracted . . . Good Lord! Adam didn't allow *those* creatures in his surgery – and a man with a heart condition.

How different from the pampered, bored matrons on whom he lavished his attentions in the comfortable Harley Street rooms.

Few of *his* patients were sick; not really sick. Their ailments, he had to admit, were often imaginary or currently fashionable. There was little wrong with most of them that a Gregory powder or a loosening of too-tight stays would not have cured in half an hour! And a good day's work spent over a wash-tub and rubbing-board would set the majority of them up for life, he thought wryly.

But they settled their large accounts promptly and without question and that, Patrick told himself as he had done so many times before, was all that mattered.

He was beginning to collect the muddle of his thoughts now. The realization that Adam had such poor patients was beginning to register.

But surely, Patrick reasoned as the pregnant woman rose clumsily to her feet and knocked almost apologetically on the surgery door, Adam must have other patients. The poor who waited so patiently on the hard benches were obviously a prop to Adam's conscience; they must surely be his 'charity' as was Aunt Hetty's perpetually bubbling wash-boiler.

He was glad when the last of them had left and a familiar voice called, 'Next, please.'

With a little smile Patrick rose to his feet, straightened his coat and gave a tweak to his cravat. Then slowly, a pulse of anticipation beating in his throat, he walked towards the door.

For a moment the face before him registered disbelief then broke into a wide, slow smile of pleasure.

'Patrick! Patrick, my dear old friend, you are here. I knew you would come!'

Adam Carmichael held out his hands, his face betraying his emotions and they stood, hands clasped, laughing with delight.

Then Patrick felt a small shock of fear for he noticed the droop of his friend's shoulders, the tired eyes and a face too thin and colourless.

'Well, doctor?'

The words sounded inept and trite but they were all Patrick could find to say. 'I think I have come in the nick of time to diagnose a severe case of over-working and to prescribe,' he said with mock severity, 'a two-week holiday in the Welsh mountains.'

Adam smiled, a yearning look fleeting across his face.

'I wish it could be possible. Sometimes, I think, I would like nothing better but I cannot leave *The Haven*.'

He stopped as a spasm of coughing shook his thin body. Then he smiled apologetically.

'But sit down, Patrick, and I will tell Sarah you have come.'

'Sarah?'

Had Adam taken a wife, then? And if he had, had she taken leave of her senses in allowing him to work so hard when it was so obvious that . . .

He shuddered inwardly and tried to shut out his thoughts but despite his long sabbatical in the Harley

Street practice, Patrick's skills had not left him. He did not like the sound of Adam's cough nor the startling decline in his appearance.

Adam smiled.

'Sarah Rigby,' he supplied. 'I don't know what we would do without her. She is a fine woman, Patrick.'

'She works at this place?'

'She *is* this place, Patrick. She drives herself without mercy.'

'As she drives you, it seems.'

'No, friend. Sarah scolds me often and says as you say that I must take a rest in the fresh air but . . .'

His voice trailed off as the rasping coughing once more caused Patrick to crease his forehead into a frown of concern.

'You are right, Adam. She says it often!'

Patrick turned to where a tall, slim young woman stood in the open doorway, a tray bearing brown mugs of steaming liquid in her hands.

'She says it so often that sometimes she tires of the sound of her own voice!'

'Ma'am.'

Patrick jumped to his feet, inclining his head in her direction.

The woman walked into the room.

'Dicky-Sam told me you had come. I have brought you a drink,' she said, handing hot cocoa to Patrick with hardly a glance in his direction. 'Molly has some meat and bread,' she said gently to Adam. 'The *Bounty* arrived this morning and there is food in the pantry again.'

'God bless the *Bounty* and the angel who sends it,' smiled Adam, 'but thank you, no. This drink will do nicely.'

He rose to his feet.

'Sarah, my dear, this is Patrick Norris. I said he would come. I knew he wouldn't fail us.'

Uneasily, Patrick remained silent, offering his hand to the tired-faced Sarah. She was, he thought, a mixture of contradictions. Her long homespun dress and white apron belied her proud bearing and the look of condescension she tossed in his direction. She wore the stamp of breeding and the garb of a servant. Her fire-red hair was scraped back from her face and tied without ceremony with a black ribbon, small wisps of it escaping to hang damply on her flushed face. She briefly offered her hand before turning once more to Adam, her blue-grey eyes tender with concern.

'Are you sure you will not eat? A little of Molly's broth, perhaps?'

'Thank you, Sarah, but no,' Adam smiled. 'I will wash my hands and put on my old jacket. Then we will take our drinks into the back parlour and talk and talk.'

He turned in the doorway and smiled again his slow gentle smile of pleasure. Then the two people in the room waited until his footsteps could be heard wearily negotiating the stairs.

'Well?' Sarah demanded, abruptly.

Patrick gazed into the strong face, gentled a little by the fine, high cheek-bones. He shrugged his shoulders.

'Doctor Carmichael is working too hard and he is not well,' he admitted.

'*Working too hard? Not well?* He is exhausted and he is sick and if you are half the doctor he says you are, sir, then you should know it!'

Patrick flushed angrily.

'I know it, ma'am.'

'Then what are you going to do about it?'

Patrick took a deep, steadying breath.

'Might I first ask, madam, who you are?' he begged the question, pointedly.

'I am Sarah Rigby and I work at *The Haven*. That is all you need to know, doctor.'

'You are employed here as a servant?'

'There are no employers and no servants in this house. We are poor and we work for the poor. We are all equal, here.'

'We?'

'Adam and Molly O'Keefe and Dicky-Sam and me.'

She gave an impatient shrug.

'But that is beside the point. Adam is coughing his lungs away!'

'Yes,' Patrick acknowledged gravely, trying hard to retain his composure, 'but that, Miss Rigby, is surely no concern of yours.'

'When one of us is sick, it is the concern of all of us,' she flung back.

Patrick shifted uneasily.

'Might I know exactly *what* your position is in this house and how you came here?' he hedged.

'You may not,' Sarah Rigby answered, flatly. 'It is sufficient to say that since society in its stupidity will not allow a woman to become a doctor, I am doing what I consider to be the next most useful thing!'

'A *woman* doctor!'

Patrick did not try to conceal the horror in his voice. 'Madam, you are . . .'

He broke off abruptly as a heavy thud was followed by a small, stifled moan.

There was a moment of frozen silence then Sarah flung her body across the room and wrenched open the door.

'Adam!'

In an instant she was on her knees beside the inert form that was huddled pathetically at the foot of the staircase.

'He's collapsed. Help me lift him,' she ordered.

Obediently Patrick placed his hands beneath Adam's slight shoulders. Without ceremony, Sarah took his feet.

'Upstairs,' she jerked, brusquely.

Carefully Patrick edged his way in the direction of Sarah's nodding head.

'The room on the right,' she panted.

Gently they laid Adam on the small bed.

'Help me get him undressed.' Already Sarah had removed Adam's cravat and unfastened the buttons of his shirt.

'*Help me!*' she demanded again as Patrick stood bemused by her flagrant disregard for convention.

Carefully they eased off the threadbare clothes.

'Here!' Sarah flung a nightshirt at Patrick. 'For God's sake, *doctor . . .*'

With heavy sarcasm she accentuated the last word, stinging Patrick into action.

'Open the window wide,' he rapped, 'this room is airless!'

Automatically his fingers searched for the pulse at Adam's wrist.

Slowly, as they stood over him rubbing his hands, the pale eyelids flickered then opened.

'Patrick?'

'Yes, Adam? I am here.'

'I'm sorry. I stumbled on the stairs.'

'You collapsed,' Sarah whispered fiercely. 'You're a fool, Adam Carmichael!'

Patrick held up his hand.

'Easy now, Adam.'

He settled the limp body more comfortably on the pillows.

'You'll be all right, now. But Miss Rigby is right, you know. You need a rest – a *long* rest.'

Meaningfully, his eyes met Adam's.

'I know, Patrick. I've known it for some time – that's why I asked you to come. I need you and my poor people need you, too. There is so much to be done and so little time . . .'

His voice whispered into silence.

'But, Adam,' Patrick felt an uneasy flush burning in his cheeks. 'I cannot . . .'

'Patrick, I *beg* of you?'

Desperately a thin, anxious hand grasped his.

'Stay for just a little while. For the sake of old times, help us?'

Patrick could not bring himself to meet the trusting eyes. He looked across the bed to where Sarah stood unmoving, asking silently for her understanding and support. He saw that the soft blue that had shaded her eyes was gone. Now they flashed a challenge of anger and contempt, grey and cold as storm-tossed waves on the river.

So this, they mocked, *is the brilliant Doctor Norris, the man who has forsaken his own and exchanged his talents for an easy living? This is the friend who will not fail us!*

Patrick caught at his breath, fighting to control the feelings that writhed inside him; feelings of shame and uncertainty, of anger and pity.

He stood, unspeaking, whipped by the scorn in Sarah Rigby's face.

'Dear friend, for pity's sake . . .?'

But Patrick Norris hardly heard Adam's gentle pleading for the steel-cold eyes that blazed into his shocked and bewildered him, so eloquent was their unspoken contempt.

Three

Suddenly in that small bare room, Patrick Norris was a child again; a bewildered, restless boy who had looked at the confining walls of the court in Lace Street and felt, almost, that they were closing in on him. He wanted to push them back with his strong young arms and shout, 'No! I won't be shut in! I will not stay in this town. Nothing shall keep me here!'

He had determined then to leave the mean streets behind him for even in his youth he vowed that Liverpool should never be allowed to hold him.

That feeling possessed him again only now it was the white walls of Adam Carmichael's sick-room that closed him in; the hand that clasped his as though it would never let it go and the fierce, unspoken challenge in Sarah Rigby's eyes.

Why, Patrick fretted, had he let this happen to him? He had been a fool to respond to Adam's letter. And how could Adam expect all men to possess his own lofty ideals?

Patrick felt a pricking of guilt, for even as the thought was born his reason destroyed it. Adam was no knight-crusader. He was a compassionate and good man; he saw what needed to be done and quietly and earnestly tried to do it.

In their youth Patrick had loved Adam as a brother. It

had amazed him that in his unreasoning obsession to rise from the poverty of Lace Street he could ever have allowed himself the luxury of such a feeling.

'Patrick?'

He felt again the tightening of fingers within his hand and because he could not again expose himself to the utter destruction of Sarah Rigby's gaze he heard himself saying.

'Very well, I will stay – for just a little while . . .'

'God bless you, Patrick,' Adam whispered, the gratitude in his voice unmistakable.

Patrick raised his head and looked into Sarah's face and for a small moment he thought that relief had replaced the animosity in her eyes.

Then he was himself again, in command of his own destiny. He would give them two days and not one hour longer and during that time he would show them what he was made of. Sarah Rigby would have to admit he was no London quack!

'You are tired, Adam,' he said. 'I will give you something to help you sleep. Perhaps if Miss Rigby will be so kind as to help me . . .'

It took all his resolve to make the request. He had not thought any woman could have made him feel so inadequate.

'Certainly, doctor, if you will come with me?'

Patrick followed her downstairs to a passage-like room that contained rows of shelves and a stone sink with a brass tap.

She coughed, apologetically.

'This was once a butler's pantry; now, it is my dispensary.'

Patrick looked around him. Home-made bandages lay neatly rolled in boxes; crude splints stood in a corner; a mortar and pestle and a few assorted jars of powders and lotions looked strangely alone in the bareness of the room.

Patrick picked up a Bunsen-burner which seemed to him to be the only concession the so-called dispensary offered to the medical advances of the nineteenth century.

'There is gas-lighting in the house, Miss Rigby?'

Sarah shook her head. 'Only in this room and in the sick-ward.'

'You have sick *here*?'

'I will show you,' Sarah nodded.

She led him into a large lofty room that must surely have once known the polite gossip of crinolined ladies Patrick mused, as they sipped a glass of Madeira or nibbled daintily on a macaroon.

Now that room was stripped bare of its elegant past, its ornately patterned wooden floor scrubbed clean of stain and polish, its occupants the sick who lay in the narrow beds that were ranged arounds its walls.

Sarah allowed only the briefest glimpse before she closed the door.

'I will take you round later when you have seen to Adam. Some of the patients will be able to leave very soon. I shall be glad of their beds, if the fever gets worse.'

Patrick quirked an enquiring eyebrow.

'The fever, ma'am?'

'Surely you knew there is cholera in the port?' Sarah replied, tersely. 'It's taking a hold near the docks.'

'And you would nurse cholera *here*?'

'If it is necessary,' Sarah shrugged. 'We try not to turn anyone away who is sick – and poor.'

Patrick turned his back abruptly. Sarah Rigby, he realized, meant every word of what she had said.

Was she, he wondered, another of that rash of ranting

women who had ideas above the capacity of their brains? What right had any woman to imagine she could be anything other than what the good God had created her for? Why couldn't women be contented to be soft and gentle; to be a comfort to the men who had chosen them in marriage and bear healthy children to carry on their name. Women, it seemed, were getting strange ideas that would have been really quite amusing had they not been so outrageously ridiculous.

Take Miss Nightingale, Patrick reasoned; a lady of good birth, yet she was bothering everybody in the medical profession for help in the training of her lady nurses.

Lady nurses?

No lady would allow herself to be subjected to the filth and squalor of infirmary wards.

No decent woman could possibly enter those stinking places; no gentlewoman could ever be a nurse! Those who set themselves up as such were dirty, dissolute creatures, didn't Sarah Rigby know that? Many of them were hopeless drunkards or part-time whores.

A *lady* nurse? It was pathetic in its stupidity and now Sarah Rigby had exceeded the bounds of credibility by saying that she wanted to become a doctor!

He reached for the laudanum bottle.

Now, how different was his Arabella, thought Patrick, absently. Arabella Harrington was a credit to womanhood. She knew her place in life and accepted it gladly. She would make him a good wife and give him children as her duty demanded.

But he had often wondered about Arabella. There was a slightness about her; a fragility that sometimes made him doubt her ability to bear a child. She was a fairy thing – an elfin ornament to grace any man's home – but how would she fare on the child-bed?

Now Sarah Rigby, Patrick's medical mind supplied, would carry her children like a barefoot peasant and give them to the world with ease and dignity. Sarah Rigby had child-bearing hips and good breasts for nursing . . .

Patrick shut down his thoughts, becoming suddenly and acutely aware of two large grey eyes that looked questioningly into his.

He felt himself flush, ashamed of his thoughts. He was betrothed to Arabella and Sarah Rigby was obviously in love with Adam Carmichael. And anyway, he asserted silently, he had only been thinking of Miss Rigby in the purest of medical terms – it was as simple as that.

In two days he would leave *The Haven* and Sarah Rigby for all time. He doubted if he would ever think about her again.

Carefully he measured a sleeping-draught, meticulously replacing the glass stopper and placing the bottle back in its place on the highest shelf.

Two days, he assured himself yet again; for just two days he would stay and take Adam's surgeries and visit his sick then he would be up and away. He would leave Liverpool gladly and without a backward glance and be damned if he would ever return!

He had been foolishly sentimental to agree to Adam's pleading but for the sake of their friendship he supposed he owed Adam something.

True, Adam was sick and needed rest and nursing, but had it not been for Sarah Rigby and the mocking scorn in her eyes, he would never have allowed himself to be coaxed into the situation at all!

Patrick gave an exclamation of annoyance, pushing the thoughts of that unspoken challenge to the back of his mind. He didn't know why he allowed the woman to disturb him so. She was of no importance and he would not think about her. He would keep out of her way and communicate with her only when he must and when he boarded the train for Harrogate he wouldn't give her another thought. Why on earth should he?

Clearing his throat with unnecessary ferocity he walked past Sarah saying coldly, 'That will be all, ma'am. I will attend to Doctor Carmichael.'

Sarah flushed with amazed outrage. How *could* he speak to her so? What right had he to dismiss her from her own dispensary as if he owned the place? What was there about the man that made Adam speak of him so lovingly?

Why, Patrick Norris was nothing but an overbearing, self-opinionated, upstart London Dandy!

She drew in a deep breath, willing herself to be calm, refusing to let him see that he had succeeded in disturbing her still further.

'As you wish, doctor,' she said, more quietly than she could ever have given herself credit for.

After all, she reasoned, he would soon tire of the endless work at *The Haven*; would quickly come to realize there was little to be made by working for the poor. The gratitude in their eyes, the satisfaction of the giving of oneself to the utmost, of fighting and sometimes winning in the face of impossible odds were the only rewards anyone could hope for.

She looked round the little room. The dispensary had been her great pride until Patrick Norris's amused eyes had forced her to admit its utter inadequacy.

They had so little money with which to buy drugs and medicines. Adam had few instruments and those he had could well have been replaced by newer, more efficient ones.

Sarah recalled the day they had decided they could

afford to buy a stethoscope. How delighted Adam had been – a child with a Christmas toy.

If only she were rich, she yearned, there would be so many things she could buy; so much more they could achieve.

Sarah sighed. Tomorrow, she must get out the account books and go through them with Molly. Together they must sort out the bills and pay those that could no longer wait.

With luck perhaps, there would be a few pounds to come from the scattering of Adam's patients who could afford to pay for treatment. There were precious few of them left. They had sold or closed their houses and taken themselves off, away from the hot, dirty streets. Only the poor remained now and they couldn't pay.

Soon there would be a stream of women down the area steps that led to Molly's kitchens, begging water from her scullery tap. At least, thought Sarah, she must be grateful that the water supply at *The Haven* was never turned on and off at will.

Water, she thought, was what the town needed most; clean, pure water for drinking and washing in and swilling the choked, stinking gutters.

She wished it would rain. There had been none for weeks, now. A good downpour would flush out the filth that helped spawn cholera; cool the sweating streets. She wondered if any new cases of the fever had been reported.

'Dear God, let it not be,' she prayed for she knew that it would be to the house in Abercromby Square that the poor wretches would come to beg help. And if it got worse, how many sick could they take in? And, come to that, how would they manage with Adam so ill?

Dear Adam, who refused to acknowledge the fact and

would work for his poor ones until his last protesting cough.

If only Patrick Norris would stay, Sarah wished. Oh, she didn't like him, but at least it would give them the chance to get Adam into the country for a few months. Rest and good clean air might help – might even cure – the consumption that was choking his lungs.

She gave a short, derisive laugh. Patrick Norris would not stay with them, she was certain of it. She was surprised that she should even have hoped that he would.

And that, thought Patrick as the last patient stammered his thanks and left the surgery, has been a good morning's work. It was a long time, he realized, since he had dealt with such a varied and interesting number of ailments. Under normal circumstances he might well have enjoyed it.

'Come in,' he called, in answer to the loud knocking.

The door opened to admit a small, limping man.

'Good morning to you, doctor.'

The weather-beaten face creased into a genuine smile of greeting.

'Begging your pardon, sir, but I was hoping to find Miss Sarah with you. She usually helps Doctor Adam with morning surgery.'

'She's not helping *me*!'

'Then she'll be down in Molly's galley, for sure.'

Patrick scowled. 'Molly's galley?'

'Miss O'Keefe's kitchens, sir. A very worthy lady is Molly O'Keefe. It's generally about this time we all has a mug o' tea, so if you'd care to accompany me, I'll be pleased to escort you.'

'Might I ask, my man, who you are?' Patrick demanded

bluntly, noticing for the first time that the chirpy little body was balanced precariously on one leg and a wooden stump attached below the knee-joint of the other.

'You may, sir, you may!'

He gave a small, comic bow, almost overbalancing in his efforts at elegance.

'Richard Samuel Pickstock, at your service.'

'Then you must be Dicky-Sam?'

'I have that honour, doctor.'

Patrick smiled. He could not find it in him to resist the cheerful good-humour that bubbled out of the man.

'You work here, I believe?'

'That I does, sir, and proud to be of service. But then, I owes me life to Doctor Adam.'

He placed his hand on his heart in a dramatic gesture.

'Carried me off the *Cornucopia* a smashed and battered wreck, they did. Fell out of the rigging I had and not one unbroken bone in me body. "Dead he'll be afore nightfall," they said, but Doctor Adam patched me up a treat – cut off me useless old leg and fitted me with a new one!'

'I see,' Patrick nodded gravely.

'So I ended me sea-days and came to work for the good doctor. Glad to be rid of that packet, I was. She's a bad ship, the *Cornucopia*, a jonah ship if ever there was one. Bad luck she's been since the day her keel was laid!'

Dicky-Sam nodded his head, sagely.

'And I'm not the only one as thinks so. Miss Sarah thinks she's a bad 'un an' all!'

The little seaman sighed, volubly. 'But I'm keeping you, sir, and you a'thirsting for a mug of char.'

He limped to the door and held it open.

'If you'd care to come along o' me, doctor . . .?'

Sarah was sitting at the large table in the basement. Beside her sat red-cheeked, black-haired Molly O'Keefe whose long dress and snow-white apron seemed to have been padded out with soft, fat cushions.

'Good morning,' Sarah greeted them without raising her head.

Dicky-Sam took two mugs from the dresser then hopped over to the blue and gold teapot that stood beside the gleaming black cooking range.

'There you are, doctor. Strong and sweet and black as Hell's kitchen!'

Molly O'Keefe stared dismally at the collection of unpaid accounts.

''Tis a terrible sight to behold, Miss Sarah. That pile of bills gets bigger every day and myself in need of soap and bathbrick,' she sighed. 'I can't cut down on cleanliness, miss.'

'No Molly, you certainly can't though I think you must eat soap, you use so much,' Sarah smiled, gently.

Then she puckered her forehead into a frown.

'We *must* pay for the coal, Molly – we need it for cooking and hot water and the coalman is so good – he gives us good weight and never charges more than sixpence ha'penny a bag.'

They were totally immersed in their business, quite unaware of the two men who sat drinking tea.

Watching Sarah unashamedly, Patrick noticed the fleeting smile, admitting reluctantly that for an instant it had transformed her face into one of rare and startling beauty.

He dropped his eyes as Sarah shut the account book with a snap and picked up two half-sovereigns that lay on the table.

She handed one to Molly O'Keefe.

'Thank you kindly, Miss Sarah.'

Molly took the small gold coin that represented her wages for the month and turned it over on her hand.

'It would please me if you would accept my contribution to the housekeeping,' she said with dignity as she returned the coin to Sarah.

Sarah inclined her head gravely.

'Thank you, Miss O'Keefe,' she returned. 'I am obliged for your kindness.'

Patrick turned to Dicky-Sam, a look of bewilderment on his face.

'Molly always does that,' Dicky-Sam whispered. 'Always gives back her wages.'

Sarah turned to the little cripple, handing him the other coin.

Dicky-Sam tipped his forelock, then opening the purse at his belt he placed the money carefully inside it, smiling cheerfully as he limped from the room.

Sarah rose to her feet, gathering up her papers.

'I'll be in the sick-ward if you need me, Molly.'

Patrick set down his mug, following closely on her heels as she climbed the narrow stairs that wound upwards from the kitchens.

In the hall Sarah paused.

'Will you take a look at Adam?' she asked.

'I have already seen him. He seems much rested,' Patrick replied. 'On no account must he be allowed up, though. He needs sleep.'

'Very well,' Sarah nodded, her eyes on the toes of her boots, 'and now, if you will excuse me . . .?'

'Miss Rigby?'

Sarah spun round. 'Yes, doctor?'

'That business of the accounts – Molly's wages, I mean. Did you have to go through all that play-acting?'

'I don't understand you.'

Sarah's chin tilted defensively but Patrick blundered blindly on.

'Why did you pay Molly her wages then take them back?'

'It pleases her.'

'Ha! I didn't notice Dicky-Sam letting you take advantage of him,' Patrick laughed. 'He was off like a shot with *his* half-sovereign. Down to the ale-house, no doubt.'

Sarah took in a deep breath.

'Doctor Norris, can you really imagine what it is like to be poor? Dicky-Sam takes his wages to the tobacconist's shop and spends it on shag and twist. He gives it to the sailors in the infirmary. It gives him pleasure, you see.'

The stubborn chin was set at defiance, the wide grey eyes narrowed into suppressed anger.

'As for Molly, I accept back her wages because it helps her to maintain her dignity. Dignity, doctor, is a rare luxury amongst the under-priviliged. Molly and Dicky-Sam are poor but they have their pride – it is all that is left to them. Would you,' she whispered, her voice trembling, 'rob them of *that*?'

For a moment they faced each other unspeaking, then Sarah said quietly, 'We eat our dinner in the kitchen at noon. I must ask you not to be late,' and without waiting for his answer she turned her back deliberately and walked into the sick-ward.

For expediency's sake, Patrick carried his mid-day meal into Adam's room and sat beside the bed to eat it. He was pleased to see the patient looking more rested and the over-bright spots of colour that had flamed in his cheeks not so pronounced.

'I feel such a fraud,' Adam protested. 'I think I will get up when I have eaten.'

'If you do,' Patrick warned with mock severity, 'I swear I shall leave!'

Adam smiled. 'You are a good friend. You must have worked hard, this morning.'

'Indeed I did but I found it most enjoyable,' Patrick replied easily with the utmost truth.

He ate his meal with relish.

'This beef stew is very good.'

'Molly is a fine cook,' Adam acknowledged. 'She came to us, destitute, a little over two years ago. She can make a meal from next to nothing and she is obsessed with cleanliness. When she is not cooking she is washing or scrubbing.'

'And Dicky-Sam?'

'Dicky-Sam was brought here quite literally to die but we were able to save him,' Adam offered modestly. 'Now he works with us at *The Haven* and I don't know what we would do at times, without his good humour.'

'*The Haven*?' Patrick mused. 'It is a strange place.'

'Perhaps it is; certainly it is strange that we have been so lucky.'

Adam set his plate aside then turned to face Patrick.

'When I could no longer pay the rent of this house I appealed to the owner for a little time. Almost at once a letter came back, saying I need make no more payments.'

'So you live rent-free? Who is your benevolent landlord?'

'You'll not believe me, Patrick, but I don't know. Once, I believe, this house belonged to a shipowner. I have tried to find his name to thank him, but I cannot.'

'You have never met him?'

'No.' Adam shook his head. 'Always my business has been with a firm of notaries. But stranger than that, Patrick, is the *Bounty*.'

Patrick nodded.

'I heard mention of it, yesterday.'

'It arrives regularly,' Adam affirmed, 'on the twenty-first day of every month.'

'And how much is this *Bounty*?'

'It is always five guineas. At first, it worried me greatly but Sarah insisted that the time to worry was when it ceased to arrive. In time I accepted it. Somewhere there is a good soul who will never know how thankful we are to him. We need the money so very much, Patrick.'

Sarah, thought Patrick. *Always, it is Sarah!*

'Ah, and there, Adam, is another mystery.'

'Sarah, you mean? A mystery? No, not really, although she came to my door one day and said simply, "I want to work with the poor and I have decided that I can best do it here." I never questioned her coming and I have never regretted it for one minute.'

'But hasn't it caused a scandal?'

Surely it must be totally unacceptable, Patrick reasoned, for two people, unrelated and unmarried to live beneath the same roof?

'Not that I ever heard of, and besides, we were well chaperoned once Molly arrived,' Adam smiled. 'Had the whole town buzzed with gossip, I do not think Sarah would have worried over-much.'

No, thought Patrick, nothing would worry Sarah Rigby except the caring for her impoverished sick.

'Do you manage to get on well with her, Adam?'

'I do indeed. She has a splendid brain. She dispenses the

medicines and takes the worry of the running of the house off my hands.'

Adam smiled tenderly.

'Sarah is a rare creature, Patrick. She is kind and compassionate – she has changed my whole life.'

'But what do you know about her other than that? Why, she may be an erring wife who has run away from her husband!'

Adam laughed and for a moment Patrick caught a glimpse of the friend of his youth.

'I do not think she has a husband although I confess I tried, once, to find out more about her. But my enquiries were always blocked and as time went on I ceased to worry. I only knew she was our dearest Sarah and that we could never manage without her. I was always one to be thankful for my blessings, and Sarah is truly a blessing.'

There was a brief knock on the door and the subject of Adam's unstinted praise walked into the room without ceremony.

'It's Margaret-Mary Haggarty,' Sarah announced shortly. 'She's in labour.'

Adam made to throw back his bed-clothes.

'I must get dressed,' he whispered. 'I must go to her.'

'No, Adam!'

Patrick placed a restraining hand on his friend's arm. 'You must stay in bed – I order it. I will see to Mrs Haggarty.'

'But it isn't as easy as that, Patrick,' Adam protested, weakly. 'Margaret-Mary is not strong; she is worn out with child-bearing. I warned her and I warned Haggarty that another child would be the death of her . . .'

He shrugged helplessly.

'All we can do now, Patrick, is to give her what help and comfort we can. She hasn't a chance, God help her!'

Four

. . . She hasn't a chance!

Inexplicably Margaret-Mary Haggarty's wellbeing was of supreme importance to Patrick.

He rose to his feet, the thought of such a challenge setting his blood racing. He had been present at a great many confinements, some of them extremely awkward ones and he'd never lost a mother in childbirth, yet. What was more, he exulted, he wasn't going to lose one now without the fight of his life!

Of Mrs Haggarty's life, he thought, ruefully. He didn't know why suddenly an unknown woman who lived in obscure poverty should cause him even a second thought. Did he, perhaps, want to show them what he was made of; that there was more to Patrick Norris than his elegantly-cut clothes?

He shrugged. He didn't have to prove anything to Adam, did he? Surely then those grey, scornful eyes couldn't be the cause of his sudden charitable love for his fellow-men?

Pah! He was being ridiculous! He was a doctor and sworn to the care of all sick. It had nothing at all to do with Sarah Rigby — absolutely nothing!

Angrily he shut down his stupid thoughts.

'Adam,' he said gently, 'I am well able to attend to your Mrs Haggarty. There'll be a midwife there, I take it?'

'Yes,' Sarah interposed, doubtfully. 'But I think it might be better if I were to come with you . . .'

'I thank you, ma'am, but that will not be at all necessary,' Patrick retorted, more firmly than he had intended. 'But if you would be so good as to prepare a laying-in bag, however, I shall be obliged to you.'

Sarah spun round on her heel, biting back the angry words that sprang to her lips. Then she shrugged her shoulders briefly and walked resignedly from the room. She mustn't upset Adam, she thought. For his sake and for *The Haven*, she must do her utmost to prevent open conflict with Patrick Norris. Nothing else, she told herself firmly, absolutely nothing else mattered.

She was waiting in the hall when Patrick came downstairs with the laying-in bag packed and his street-coat and top hat at the ready to hand to him.

'Mrs Haggarty lives in Cable Street. I could come with you if you wished,' she said hopefully 'and show you the quickest way there?'

'Thank you, Miss Rigby. I am grateful to you, but I shall manage quite well alone.'

Damn the woman and her insistence he thought angrily as he walked in the direction of St John Street. Didn't she realize, he fumed, that he knew every alley and back street in the town?

Of necessity he slowed down his steps and breathed in the stifling mid-day air, wondering what he would find when he reached the house in Cable Street. He turned as he heard he heard a familiar voice calling his name.

'Patrick! Wait for me!'

It was the first time Sarah had used his name and it added to his annoyance that he should feel pleasure.

'You need not have bothered yourself, ma'am,' he said formally. 'I assure you I am well able to manage.'

Sarah shrugged her shoulders.

'Nevertheless, I would like to be with Mrs Haggarty,' she said quietly. 'She knows and trusts Adam but you will be a stranger to her. It is best – truly it is – that I should come with you.'

Matching her step to Patrick's she strode easily by his side, neither of them speaking again until they reached Cable Street.

The wretched little huddle of houses was all Patrick remembered from his youth, built into a small, airless court with rubbish-strewn gutters and filthy pavements.

On the steps of the Haggarty house sat six children the eldest of whom – a girl – Patrick supposed to be not more than ten years old. She rose to her feet as they approached.

'Hullo, miss,'

Shyly she addressed Sarah.

'I'm glad you've come. I'm awful afeard. Me Ma's terrible badly.'

Sarah placed her arm round the thin shoulders.

'It'll be all right,' she comforted. 'Doctor Norris will take good care of your Ma.'

Large brown eyes looked unwaveringly into Patrick's.

'She didn't want you. She asked for Doctor Adam.'

'Doctor Adam isn't very well,' Sarah explained gently, 'but Doctor Norris is a fine London doctor, really he is!'

'He'll not let Ma die, will he, miss?'

'Silly girl, of course not! What an awful thing to think!' Sarah replied with more conviction than she felt.

She fished into the pocket of her skirt.

'See, here is a penny. How would you all like to share a bag of humbugs?'

'Oooh!'

For the first time the too-old eyes came alive and

hitching the youngest of the children onto her hip with an ease born of long practice the girl seemed momentarily to forget her fears.

'Thanks, miss,' she breathed, and calling the little brood around her she hurried them away in search of so rare a treat.

'Poor little wench,' Sarah sighed as she watched the bare feet skimming the hard, uncaring pavements. 'She's never had time to be a child . . .'

Margaret-Mary Haggarty was laid on a hard wooden bed, moaning softly into her pillow when Patrick pushed open the door of the downstairs room.

A small fire sulked in the hearth and a pan of water had been set there to boil.

Beside it, in the only chair, a woman rocked comfortably, a piece of knitting between her dirty fingers. By her side on the hearth stood a half-empty bottle.

She glanced up with disinterest as they entered.

'Good day to ye, Mistress Rigby. And who's the fine young feller ye've brought with ye?'

Insolently her eyes searched Patrick from head to foot.

'I am a doctor, madam,' Patrick replied stiffly.

The old woman bared her toothless gums in a gin-sodden leer.

'Well, my pretty, ye're wasting your time,' she nodded towards the bed. 'I'll have this stocking finished afore that one gets rid of her burden.'

'Who is this . . . creature?' Patrick ground, turning angrily to Sarah.

'She's the midwife, but if I had my way,' Sarah made no attempt to lower her voice, 'I'd not let her within a mile of a laying-in!'

Patrick walked quietly to the hearth and picking up the gin bottle thrust it at the woman.

'Out!' he rapped, jerking his head towards the door. 'Out, you dirty old rag-bag and take your bottle with you!'

His face glowered scarlet with rage.

'. . . And if I catch you again at a child-bed,' he yelled after the retreating figure, 'I'll fling you into the Mersey!'

Shaking his head he turned to Sarah.

'That's not enough water. Can you get more?'

'I'll try,' she replied doubtfully from the doorway, 'but have a look at Mrs Haggarty. I'm afraid for her,' she added, her voice low.

Patrick took off his coat then bent over the frightened woman who lay paralysed with pain on the rickety bed.

Taking her hand he said gently, 'Hullo, Mrs Haggarty. I've come to help you. Everything will be all right, now.'

'Doctor Adam?' The tired eyes registered apprehension. 'Where's Doctor Adam?'

'Doctor Adam has a sickness, ma'am, but Miss Rigby and I will take good care of you. I'm Doctor Norris,' he smiled.

The woman's reply was lost in a cry of pain. For a moment her body jerked and writhed then, gasping for breath she whispered, 'I'm terrible afeard, sir. You'll not let me die? For the sake of the bairns . . .?'

Patrick squeezed her hand reassuringly.

'If I do, Mrs Haggarty, you'll be the first mother I've lost on the child-bed.'

He smiled gently into her terror-filled eyes.

'Trust me?' he urged.

He looked at her frail, ugly body and cheeks sunken in a face made old before its time.

By God, he vowed, you shall *not* die, you poor creature.

He took a long sobering breath. He had never needed the Almighty's help more than he was going to need it now for Adam had been right, Patrick realized. Only a small miracle was going to save Margaret-Mary and her unborn child.

He tried to smile courage into her heart, to will his strength into her, to urge her to fight.

'All right, Mrs Haggarty?' he whispered. 'You and me together – we'll manage, eh?'

Sarah moved aside the pan and set the half-filled bucket precariously to boil.

'I couldn't get much water,' she apologized, 'there was barely a trickle from the tap but it'll do to be going on with.'

There had been three women waiting at the stand-tap but they'd gladly given her precedence.

'Here ye are, Miss Sarah.'

The precious liquid had been tipped into her bucket.

'Take my water, and welcome to it.'

'Bless you,' Sarah had whispered, grateful to be spared the agonizing wait.

Hell! she thought. This town is a small hell! No water, no food – no hope. It is a place to be endured for only as long as it takes a body to find the means to get out of it!

Where would it all end? she thought as she opened the laying-in bag.

She took out aprons for herself and Patrick then threw twinning-string and scissors into the pan of hot water.

'And please God we'll need them,' she prayed silently walking to Patrick's side.

'How is she?'

'The child should have been born hours ago,' his voice was low. 'Did you pack the instruments?'

Sarah shook her head.

'We have none.'

'No instruments? But the woman needs help! She is spent and her heart is . . .'

Patrick shrugged. He might have known it. He thought fleetingly of London and the women who were confined in comparative comfort and complete safety; women who could be helped through their pains with chloroform.

But this was Cable Street and there was nothing at all with which to help Margaret-Mary Haggarty. Why, oh why, he fumed, had he left his own bag in Harley Street? But then, he'd been going on holiday, hadn't he?

How on earth he wondered, did Adam achieve so much with so little to help him? Now, if something were not done quickly the patient would indeed die. It was as desperate as that.

Patrick spun round as a knocking on the outer door interrupted his angry thoughts.

'Here's another bucket of water for ye, Miss Sarah,' a voice whispered. 'And how is the poor woman doin'?'

'I hope she will be all right,' Sarah replied quietly. 'Doctor Norris will do all he possibly can.'

'Ah, but 'twould be a mercy if the good Lord took her so it would, for what's to become of her with Haggarty not cold in his grave?'

'Haggarty dead?' Sarah gasped.

'Did ye not know then, Miss Rigby? Got himself into a drunken fight on the quayside. Fished him out of George's Basin they did, four days back and the shock of it all starts Margaret-Mary in labour three weeks before her time!'

Sarah closed her eyes wearily, unable to trust herself to speak.

'Well, miss, there's one thing to be thankful for,' the woman continued. 'If Mistress Haggarty comes out of this with her life at least 'tis the last time she'll have to endure the child-bed! Haggarty was a lustful man when the drink was on him, God rest his drunken soul!'

Sarah was grateful for the water but she was impatient to be away.

'Thank you, ma'am, for your kindness,' she whispered, still shocked by the awful news.

'I'll fetch ye more, miss, if they don't turn the water off again!'

'Bless you,' Sarah smiled, quietly closing the door behind her.

She turned to Patrick.

'Did you hear that?'

'I did!'

Grimly he nodded his head.

By God, but the poor woman should not die! He took a deep breath, cold and calm again.

Desperate straits needed desperate measures, didn't they?

Squaring his shoulders he walked back to the bedside.

'Mrs Haggarty?'

Wearily the head turned on the pillow and fear-filled eyes looked pleadingly into Patrick's.

He closed his eyes briefly, flinching inwardly as he hit her. He felt his knuckles rasp against the defenceless chin and for an instant he wanted to vomit.

'Patrick!'

Sarah flung herself to his side, eyes wide with horror.

Dropping on her knees at the bed-side she looked up at him as if he had lost all reason.

'For pity's sake are you mad? You've knocked her senseless!'

Patrick grasped Sarah's shoulders, pulling her to her feet, shaking her roughly.

'Listen to me . . .'

He forced her to meet his eyes.

'You're right; she's unconscious and we've got just about three minutes before she comes round. Now, go to the other side of the bed and do exactly as I tell you!'

Suddenly Sarah felt calm, every vestige of tension gone. It seemed as if Patrick's personality had taken over completely, exuding confidence, silently urging her to have faith, to trust him.

'Take her legs,' he said quietly. 'Bend them towards the abdomen and press gently . . . gently . . .'

Sarah did as she was told, watching fascinated the probing fingers and hands that skilfully eased and manipulated.

She heard a muttered '*Good!*' and saw with relief that the tiny head was already supported on Patrick's hand.

For a moment it seemed that the whole of the world held its breath then unbelievably the child lay on the bed.

Briefly Sarah felt a surge of joy, searching with her eyes for Patrick's so that they might share his triumph.

But there was no elation in Patrick's face for the baby's body, Sarah realized, bore an unhealthy grey pallor and its limbs were limp and unmoving.

'String!' Patrick rapped. 'Two pieces – and scissors!'

Deftly he separated the child from its mother then held the prostrate little form aloft.

From the set of Patrick's face, Sarah knew that all was not well. Beseechingly her eyes met his, begging him silently to tell her that her fears were unfounded.

'I don't know,' he answered her unspoken question. 'The infant is in deep shock. The umbilical cord was wrapped round its neck . . .'

Gently he inserted a finger into the little mouth, hooking out mucus.

'I can't get a heart-beat or a pulse,' he muttered half to himself as he slapped the baby's back.

From the bed came a low moan as Mrs Haggarty struggled out of the blackness that had been her salvation.

'Lie still, Mrs Haggarty,' Patrick ordered sitting on the edge of the bed, suspending the child head downwards over his knee.

Gently, expertly, he began to massage the cold little back, helping and willing the lungs to start their breathing, urging as he did so the still and unresponding heart to beat.

For a while there was silence in the hot room, a quiet that seemed to scream out with tension and despair.

Patrick closed his eyes.

He is praying, thought Sarah, and it is all we can do, now.

Please God, she joined her unspoken entreaties to his, *let this little babe live?*

Desperately she watched, unwilling to lift her eyes from Patrick's hands.

Please, oh please try! she willed her strength into the inert little form. She couldn't bear it now if the child died. Not after Margaret-Mary had suffered so much; not after Patrick had worked so hard, so very skilfully.

She heard a small choking cough and Patrick's eyes jerked upwards to hers, his hands redoubling their efforts.

Then there was a cry, weak but unmistakable and Patrick felt a movement beneath his hands.

With a shout he grasped the little ankles, holding the child aloft again, slapping its back, its buttocks and its legs.

'Come on then, little one,' he coaxed. 'Try . . .'

The limp arms stiffened then flailed the air; the back arched protestingly, relaxed then arched again. The child spluttered and coughed, then gasping the life-giving air into its lungs, angrily bawled itself into life.

Patrick threw back his head and laughed out loud.

'Mistress Haggarty,' he cried triumphantly, 'you have a fine boy!'

Then he handed the child to Sarah and stood gravely looking down at the woman.

She grasped his hand in hers.

'I'm alive?' she whispered, tears spilling from her eyes. 'It's all over?'

Patrick nodded, smoothing the damp hair from her brow with gentle hands.

'I'm sorry I had to hit you.'

Expertly he ran his fingers over her jaw. 'We had so little time – I had to do it. Believe me, ma'am, there was no other way.'

Margaret-Mary smiled through her tears.

'God love ye, doctor, it's not the first time I've had a fist in me face,' she whispered, 'and never before in such a good cause; never at all . . .'

She took his hand and laid it to her cheek.

'Bless you,' she said simply then held out her arms for her son.

Slowly Sarah and Patrick walked home to Abercromby Square.

Patrick's body ached with fatigue. His shirt clung damply to his back, his coat hung carelessly over his arm and he had no idea what had become of his silk cravat. The elegant doctor from Harley Street looked more like a man toiling home after a hard day's labour but he was smiling.

'Imagine,' he said with undisguised pride, 'Mrs Haggarty calling the baby after me?'

Shyly she had asked his name.

'Patrick, is it? And 'tis a good Irish name. I'll be calling this bairn for you then, sir, for don't we both owe our lives to you?'

'Patrick Haggarty,' he grinned down at Sarah. 'It sounds good, eh?'

Then suddenly he was serious.

'I had to do it – hit Mrs Haggarty, I mean. That poor face will be black and blue before long!'

'You had no choice,' Sarah comforted 'and I think it hurt you more than it hurt Margaret-Mary.'

'I could have broken her jaw, though,' Patrick insisted ruefully.

'You could have but you didn't,' Sarah insisted. 'Forget it. The end justified the means and anyway, think how pleased Adam will be when we tell him the news.'

Then she frowned.

'Though what will become of them all now with Haggarty dead, God only knows.'

'Will she not go back to her own people in Ireland?'

'Ireland!' Sarah retorted bitterly. 'She can just as easily starve here! No,' she shrugged, 'it will be either the streets or the workhouse. Like as not it'll be the workhouse. Margaret-Mary isn't one to take to prostitution.'

Patrick noticed that Sarah's face was unbelievably sad as she spoke and he knew what she was thinking.

Against all odds he had snatched a mother and her baby from almost certain death. He had felt proud when she whispered, 'You've saved us both'.

But for what he wondered grimly as he walked up the steps of the house in Abercromby Square, had he saved them?

'I'll go and tell Adam,' Sarah called as she hurried up the staircase.

Patrick nodded briefly to the men and women who waited patiently on the benches ranged round the hall.

He had hardly taken his seat behind Adam's desk when there was a loud and urgent knocking on the door.

'I'll be seeing Doctor Adam, for it's life and death, so it is!' demanded a woman's strident voice.

Patrick rose to his feet.

'What is it? What is wrong?'

'It's Doctor Adam I'm wanting, sir. Would you be telling me where I can find him, for this poor old body here . . .'

She indicated the small, frail woman who lolled, eyes closed, on the bench.

' . . . she's powerful sick. How I got her here I'll never know for if you ask me she's dying on her feet!'

Patrick's eyes opened wide with horror. For a moment he was incapable of speech. Then he heard his voice, strange and far away, '*Aunt Hetty!*'

Desperately he scooped the pathetic form into his arms, his heart hammering loudly in his ears.

Aunt Hetty *dying*? he thought, wildly.

'Sarah!' he called as he ran towards the stairs. 'Sarah! Where are you?'

Her name had come easily to his lips but he did not notice it.

Five

Sarah ran along the landing; she had heard the brief commotion and sensed the urgency in Patrick's voice. Now, a glance at his face confirmed her fears.

'Miss Hetty!'

She looked at the frail old woman whose grey head rested beneath Patrick's chin.

'Patrick, what is the matter?'

'I don't know,' he panted, half turning towards the woman who had brought his aunt to *The Haven* and who now followed closely on his heels.

'Why did you bring her here?' he demanded, furiously. 'This place is a charity, for the *poor*!'

'And where else would I take her and what is she but poor?' the woman retorted.

Sarah held open the door of her own room.

'In here. Put her in my bed.'

Quietly and efficiently, as if it were an everyday occurrence, Sarah turned down the bed-clothes and Patrick was grateful that there was no accusation in her eyes, no triumphant condemnation.

He stood by silently as she gently removed his aunt's boots and unfastened the buttons of her blouse.

'What is the matter with Miss Norris do you think?'

Sarah turned to quietly ask the woman who hesitated

in the doorway still, anxious and curious. 'Why did you bring her here?'

'Who else would have taken her in will you tell me?' the woman asked, her face sullen. 'It was either *The Haven* or the workhouse!'

'What do you mean?' Patrick rasped, his fingers searching for the pulse-beat at the old woman's wrist. 'What do you mean, ma'am – the *workhouse*?'

Hostile now, the woman fixed Patrick with a long, cold stare.

'Have ye not heard of the place, my pretty?' she mocked. 'It's a house of charity where they take you when there's nowhere else for you to starve!'

'Starve?' Patrick jerked.

'Aye *starve*. Maybe you'll not know the meaning of the word but when an old woman goes without food she gets hungry and what with all the washing and Black Becky's tallyman . . .'

'See now, mistress.'

Gently Sarah took the woman's arm.

'I am very grateful for your kindness, but could you come downstairs with me? You can tell me all about it whilst the doctor sees to Miss Norris, can't you? I'd be very glad if you would,' she coaxed.

Patrick breathed heavily, fighting to control his anger, grateful for Sarah's intervention.

'Aunt Hetty?' he whispered, when they were alone. 'It's all right now. I'll take care of you.'

Desperately he rubbed the work-worn old hands.

Starving? His mind was bemused. Aunt Hetty paying money to the tallyman? It couldn't be true?

But a mere glance at the ashen face, the sunken cheeks and the thin, gaunt body told him his fears were stark reality.

With relief he saw a flickering of her eyelids and for an instant the old eyes gazed upwards then closed again as if they were unwilling to look on the bleak, uncaring world.

'Aunt Hetty?'

Patrick felt frail nervous fingers groping for his.

'Is it you, boy?'

'Yes, Aunt. Don't worry. You'll be all right, now.'

He lifted her gnarled hand, his fingertips searching again for a pulse-beat. It shocked him to find it was so very weak and irregular.

'What on earth have you been up to?' he asked, indulgently, his lips close to her ear. 'Is it true you've been neglecting yourself – not eating properly?'

'An old body like mine doesn't need so much inside it . . .'

Her voice trailed off into a tired whisper.

Guiltily Patrick remembered that not so very long ago his aunt had said those same words. She had said them as she sat at the table watching him eat. She gave me her supper, he thought, with a dull flush of shame. The plate of brawn, he remembered, that he'd forced himself to eat had probably represented the whole of her food for the day.

'If I can rest for a while I'd be grateful. It's the heat, you see . . .'

'You will rest until you are well, Aunt Hetty', Patrick asserted, firmly.

For an instant the ghost of the woman she had once been wraithed across Hetty Norris's face and she opened her mouth as if to protest.

But she did not. Nodding her head she said resignedly, 'Yes, I think I would like that.'

It was becoming obvious to Patrick that most probably there was little wrong with his aunt that bed-rest and good food would not eventually cure but his anxiety could still not be disguised as he asked, 'Do you think you could try to eat a little?'

'Yes, boy, just a little . . . I'll try . . .'

'I won't be long.'

Patrick walked towards the door.

'Now stay there, Aunt Hetty . . .'

He hesitated, his hand on the door-latch, fearful lest when he returned she would have vanished.

Hetty Norris smiled.

'I will, Patrick, I will.'

Gulping a deep breath of relief into his lungs, Patrick gently closed the door then hurried once more in search of Sarah.

'How could I have been so blind?' Patrick whispered, 'so inexcusably stupid?'

Sarah was in the kitchen, heating a pan of milk.

'How is your aunt?'

'Oh, I don't know what to think.'

Patrick shook his head wearily. 'I can't bring myself to believe what my own common sense tells me is true. How could she have got so ill? Why didn't I notice it the other day, Sarah? What was I about?'

He sat down on a hard wooden chair then jumped to his feet again, pacing the floor as he spoke.

'I mean, I had no idea — and there's the tally-man . . .'

He shook his head.

'How could she have got herself into Rebecca Solomon's clutches?'

'I don't know, Patrick. I can only tell you what her neighbour told me. It seems your aunt is deeply in debt and has to take in washing to keep up the payments. It's a terrible thing, but when Black Becky's tallyman gets a hold, a body might as well give up!'

'But why didn't she let me know? Do you think I'd have seen her in want?'

Sarah did not reply and Patrick had the grace to feel shame for his letters to his aunt had been few and far between, of late. And he should have known, he thought in savage self-condemnation, that those of Hetty Norris's breed didn't whine. Hetty Norris and those like her were a proud lot.

But for all that, Patrick conceded, his aunt was in need of nursing, now.

'Look, Sarah,' he hesitated, 'I'd be grateful if Aunt Norris could stay here for just a few days until I can sort things out.'

Sarah smiled.

'Of course she can stay. She must stay until she is well and strong again. Don't worry, we'll take care of her.'

Patrick stammered his thanks.

'And do you think you could find something for her to eat? A little beef-tea or some calves-foot jelly, perhaps? Something light and nourishing?'

Sarah shook her head.

'I'm sorry, Patrick, but we have neither of those things. I thought perhaps some bread and milk –'

She nodded towards the pan.

'You have nothing more suitable?'

'No, nothing at all. Tomorrow, perhaps . . .'

'But is there no meat at all in the house? Some of the beef stew we ate at dinner would be adequate?'

'It is all gone. Oh, we did have a little meat but we gave it to Adam because he is sick and to you, because you are a guest,' Sarah acknowledged, lamely.

'But what do *you* eat, then?'

'Oh, we manage. Some of our patients pay in kind, if they can. We eat well when the butcher's rheumatism bothers him,' she smiled impishly, 'or the flour-miller's gout plays him up. And there's a farmer who pays his bill in milk and eggs!'

'But is there nothing at the moment for my aunt, other than bread and milk?'

'I'm sorry, Patrick,' she shook her head, sadly. 'But tomorrow we may be lucky. Perhaps someone, somewhere, will give us something. I hope so, for the ward is full.'

Patrick's face flushed a deep and angry red.

'I'm going out for a while,' he jerked, tersely.

'But Patrick, your aunt,' Sarah stammered.

'Take her the bread and milk and stay with her, will you? I'll not be long!'

Angrily he brushed past her, his eyes downcast. How could he have been so stupid and selfish and utterly uncaring, he wondered, slamming the front door behind him.

Sarah's words spun giddily in his brain.

' . . . *once the tallyman gets a hold . . . only bread and milk – maybe tomorrow . . .*'

Tomorrow. Elusive tomorrow! Well, perhaps now, just for once he thought, he could do something *today*; something that might help even the score!

Still trembling with anger, with shock and shame, he strode purposefully towards Lord Street and Mr Gaunt's select emporium. And when, his conscience sitting a little easier within him he left the shop and set out for *The Haven* again, his thoughts were even yet in a turmoil of uncertainty and muddle.

He had always wanted to become a doctor, he mused, and a good doctor into the bargain. One day, he had vowed, he would take his place amongst the London physicians and surgeons, learned and respected as they were. And he had reached London far more easily than he could have hoped, for it had been offered to him on a plate.

Less than a month after facing a London Board of Examiners he had returned to the city of his ambitions, assistant to the famous Doctor Harrington and a whole new world of medicine within his grasp. He had achieved all that yet had failed to recognize that his own aunt was under-nourished, to say the least!

Shamefully he wrenched his thoughts away from the frail little body of Hetty Norris.

If only one small part of the resources of the London practice were available at Abercromby Square, he thought; if there had been even the barest of necessities at his command, the Haggarty baby need not have come into the world in so dramatic a way and at so terrible a risk.

Patrick thought again of Sarah, wondering how often she needed to go hungry.

Sarah had been magnificent; he couldn't have managed at Mrs Haggarty's without her help. Perhaps he had been wrong about her, he thought. Maybe she *was* one of the rare ones – a truly dedicated woman. Almost certainly she was, or why did she put up with the intolerable conditions that existed at *The Haven*? Could it be that she and Adam . . .?

He tried to wrest his thoughts away from what did not concern him but it was difficult not to think of Adam and his struggle against poverty and sickness and greed.

Adam had no well-stocked dispensary. His patients could not afford to pay large fees. Some of them could not pay at all . . .

Adam Carmichael made the best of the little he had and gave of himself in unstinted measure. He was a doctor against all odds and in the truest sense of the word.

Adam was also a very sick man. He needed rest, freedom from worry and above all he needed good, nourishing food.

'. . . *maybe tomorrow* . . .'

No, not tomorrow, Patrick insisted, quickening his steps into Abercromby Square. For just this one time, they would have food today!

'A sixpenny-piece for you lad,' he'd said to the boy with the handcart, 'if you can get this load delivered to number 13, Abercromby Square in five minutes time!'

The boy had earned his sixpence, Patrick exulted for Molly's excited voice could be heard exclaiming, 'Why, Miss Sarah, it's a miracle! Will ye look at that great pile? A sack of flour, eggs, bacon . . .'

'Tea, sugar, mutton, sausages . . .!' Sarah took up the chant.

'Potatoes, butter, oatmeal – oh, miss, there must be a catch in it. It's all a mistake – it must be?'

'No mistake,' Patrick said quietly from the doorway.

Sarah spun round, her eyes shining, her cheeks flushed.

'You, Patrick? You've paid for all this food? But why? *Why?*'

Her eyes danced with happiness.

'Because there was nothing in the larder,' Patrick shrugged, 'because Aunt Hetty is hungry and Adam is sick.'

He smiled into Sarah's eyes.

'See they are both well-fed, will you? See that all of them are!'

Then abruptly, as if ashamed of his generosity, he strode towards the door.

'I'll take another look at Adam then I'll be with Aunt Hetty if I'm wanted,' he said, tersely.

Without a backward glance, he left them.

Doctor Robert Harrington ate his roast beef with obvious enjoyment but his daughter toyed petulantly with the food on her plate.

'But, Papa,' she pouted, 'Patrick *promised*. He promised to join us within three days at the most. He should have been here, by now!'

'Three days, four days – what does it matter, Arabella?'

'It matters to *me*, Papa. It matters a great deal to me. I am bored. I am quite, quite bored!'

She waved away the waiter who removed her plate and offered strawberries and thick, whipped cream.

'I am becoming tired also of visiting the Pump Room and drinking that evil-tasting water!'

'That evil-tasting water, missy, is extremely beneficial. I am sorry you are bored and I am not a little hurt that you are not grateful for my concern for your health.'

There were times, sighed Doctor Harrington inwardly, when he found his daughter's behaviour a little trying.

True, there was no one to blame, he supposed but himself. He had spoiled her outrageously. His dear wife had never recovered from the child-bed and Arabella had been all that was left to him to lavish his riches and affection upon.

He had been pleased when young Patrick had haltingly asked for his daughter's hand in marriage. Patrick was a good doctor; he had indeed the makings of a brilliant physician. Robert Harrington had been glad to give the safekeeping of Arabella's future to so worthy a man.

But were they really suited, he pondered.

That Patrick was fond of Arabella Doctor Harrington did not doubt, but was Arabella ready for marriage to *any* man?

All her life she had been sheltered and indulged. Without so much as a thought she could spend on one gown what would have fed a family for a whole week.

Had he, wondered Robert Harrington, been too kind, tried too hard to make recompense to Arabella for the loss of her dear mama?

'You are not listening to me, Papa. You do not care that I am unhappy and pining away for Patrick.'

'Dearest child, Patrick will have good reason for his prolonged stay in Liverpool. He wished to see his aunt, remember, and no doubt he will have friends to visit. Be patient, little dove. Patrick will come soon.'

'I cannot be patient, Papa. My patience has become exhausted!'

Arabella's bottom lip trembled dangerously. She reminded him, thought her father, of a child who agitated for a toy, thinking she had only to snap her fingers and it would be hers. Arabella knew nothing of pain or suffering and the world outside her. She was like a small nestling, ever demanding food and it was he, her own father, who must accept the blame.

He had given in to her every whim and unless something were done about it and soon, there would be nothing but unhappiness ahead for Arabella. Patrick, decided Doctor Harrington, would not countenance such behaviour for long after they were married.

If only, he thought, he could find the moral courage to give his fledgling a push. Hadn't she been sheltered too long in the nest of love and indulgence he had so foolishly built around her?

Glancing up he saw that tears were imminent and knew at all costs he must avoid another of Arabella's tantrums in the crowded dining-room of the hotel.

'Well, little love,' he said with forced jocularity, 'if Doctor Norris will not come to Miss Arabella then Arabella must go to her beloved!'

Arabella blinked her tears away with a start. Surely Papa could not be serious?

How could she go to Patrick? It was not possible for her to travel without a chaperon to Liverpool and it would not be proper for a young lady to run after a gentleman, even accepting that gentleman was her bethrothed. Papa was teasing her again. He was humouring her as if she were a child and she *wasn't* a child. She was nearly nineteen and soon she would be a married lady.

Angry now, Arabella dropped her eyes to the table. If only her father would treat her as an adult, she wished. If only she could convince him she was no longer his little girl; that she had a mind and a heart and a will of her own.

If Patrick would not come to her?

Deliberately she folded her napkin.

'May I be excused, Papa?' she asked and walked purposefully from the room.

Robert Harrington gazed with affection at his daughter's retreating back.

Poor little Arabella, he thought. It had been wrong of him to say such a thing, even in jest, but at least Arabella had sufficient good sense to know he had only been teasing. And it had at least had the effect of drying her tears, of avoiding a most unpleasant scene . . .

He sighed. He would give her time to compose herself and when he had finished his meal and sipped a glass of port, Arabella would be her usual sweet self again and they would be the best of friends once more.

Smiling indulgently, Doctor Robert Harrington reached for the decanter.

Patrick tapped out his pipe on the heel of his boot, reluctant to return to the house but knowing he must.

He looked across the unkempt garden to where honey-suckle twined itself round a marble figure, where tufts of weeds choked once immaculate paths and roses ran a sweet riot of neglect.

Where was he now, thought Patrick, that benevolent owner to whom the rent of this great house meant so very little?

His gaze travelled beyond the decaying summerhouse to where Dicky-Sam had planted cabbages and potatoes.

How did a one-legged man manage to till a garden? What a painstaking labour of love the vegetable plot must be.

Patrick's mouth quirked into a smile. What a grand little character the ex-seaman was. Only that morning he had sidled into *The Haven* kitchens, his pockets stuffed with large green apples. He had found them by the canal basin. They had fallen, he explained, his face wreathed in innocence, from the back of a farmer's cart!

And Milly had called him a thievin' wee divil and promptly sprinkled the apples with sugar and popped them into the fire-oven to bake, thanking the good Lord for his providence as she did so and asking a pardon whilst she was about it for Dicky-Sam Pickstock and his itching fingers!

What a strange pair they made, Patrick mused; how great their simple hearts.

A soft footfall caused him to turn and Sarah stood beside him.

'I thought I might find you here,' she said quietly, sitting without ceremony on the stone steps at his feet. 'I often steal a few minutes in the garden at nightfall.'

She had been washing her hair and it hung loose and damp, almost to her waist.

Patrick had never seen her with her hair free for she always wore it in a severe utilitarian bun in the nape of her neck.

Glancing down he saw that the top buttons of her dark blouse were unfastened and with a surge of delight wondered why he had never before noticed the vulnerable curve of her slender neck.

Now, as she softly towelled the ends of her hair the gathering twilight gentled the care from her face and Patrick realized for the first time the serenity of her beauty.

For a moment he stood enchanted, a small pulse beating at his throat whilst the scent of honeysuckle drifted over them.

There was so much he wanted to say to her in this moment of tranquillity. He wanted to thank her for her help and support when he had been almost sick with worry at the Haggarty house; he wanted to thank her for taking in Aunt Hetty and for not censuring him for his callous neglect; he wanted to tell her of the turmoil that raged inside him, demanding that he choose between love and duty. Love for his aunt and Adam; duty to his employer and Arabella.

But he could not discuss Arabella with Sarah. It would be disloyal and he knew in his heart that he did not want to. He did not want to break their private little peace. He wanted to remember always the utter stillness that heralded the July night; a stillness so complete that he felt he could reach out with his hand and touch it as it folded itself like deep blue velvet over the harshness of the town. He wanted to keep in his heart for all time the earthy smell of grass touched briefly with evening dew, of honeysuckle scent mingling with the perfume of damask roses and of a woman who sat at his feet with newly-washed hair.

But Patrick's small moment of enchantment was not to last for Dicky-Sam's urgent call shattered the peace of the garden.

'Miss Sarah? Doctor Patrick? Be anybody there?'

'Here, Dicky,' called Sarah.

The little man tip-tapped down the path.

'Somebody'll have to go quick to Leather Lane, miss! Terrible carnage, there's been!'

'A fight?'

'Aye. Started over a street woman. Some seamen from the *Cornucopia*, so I heard tell.'

Patrick heard the quick hiss of Sarah's indrawn breath.

'Where is it?' he asked.

'The Compass, sir, and a right brothel of a place it is, begging your pardon, Miss Sarah!'

Sarah rose to her feet. 'Is it bad, then?'

'It is an' all! They've wrecked the tap-room. Whole thing seems to have got out of hand.'

'Right. I'll go!'

Even as he spoke, Patrick was making for the house.

'Wait for me! I'll come with you.'

'No, Sarah!' Patrick spun round in his tracks. 'It's no fit place for a woman. Stay and keep an eye on Aunt Hetty and Adam. And send the patients away unless there's something really urgent. Ask them to come back in the morning.'

Dicky-Sam limped out of the surgery holding Adam's bag in his hand.

'I'll follow behind, sir, if you don't mind. Can't keep up along o' you with me old peg-leg.'

'Thanks, Dicky.'

Patrick took the bag, his face grim.

Running into the square, trying to recall the alleys and short-cuts that would take him towards the river-front he saw a cab slowly clip-clopping its way across Oxford Street.

Thankfully Patrick hailed the driver.

'Leather Lane,' he called, 'and quick as you can make it!'

He leaned back against the soft upholstery, the smell of leather and saddle-soap strangely comforting. He closed his eyes. He had not realized how utterly spent he was.

How, he wondered wearily did Sarah and Adam endure it, day after day, after day . . .

Six

It wasn't hard to find the Compass tavern for the brawl had spilled out into the gutters.

Running up the narrow alley Patrick sidestepped the heaving mass of cursing, sweating bodies and made for the low doorway of the inn.

From nowhere it seemed, an arm shot out level with his eyes, blocking his way.

'Let me in!' he demanded looking up into the pock-marked face of a giant of a man. 'Let me pass; I'm a doctor.'

'Git!'

Tersely the man stabbed a thumb in the direction of the bottom of Leather Lane.

'We wants no doctors, 'ere!'

'I was sent for – someone is hurt! Will you please let me in?'

''Arry!' His eyes did not leave Patrick's face for an instant, 'There's a toff 'ere says he's a doctor!'

'Who is he?'

'Wot's yer name, me pretty?'

'Norris. I'm Doctor Norris.'

'Say's he called Norris,' called the ugly one.

'Never 'eard of 'im. Tell 'im to scarper!'

'You 'eard 'im, *doctor*. 'Arry don't know yer.'

The evil-looking face thrust itself dangerously close to Patrick's.

'So sling yer hook afore someone treads on yer toes!'

The small huddle of children that looked up at Patrick found him infinitely more interesting than the fight they had been watching, sensing his strangeness, wondering at the fine cut of his clothes. Then, as if some inbred gutter-instinct told them he was not of their breed, they simultaneously linked hands and ringed him round, prancing on dirty unshod feet, eager to join the ugly one in the baiting of the stranger who dared thrust himself into a private fight.

'*Cor, luk at 'him, luk at him,*
Chuck a bit o' muck at him!'

This is madness! thought Patrick wildly.

'Will you let me in, man?' he called, vainly trying to break the barrier of tightly-clasped hands.

'*Oh, luk at him . . .!*'

The derisive chant rose higher and louder.

'No, me fine cock-bird. You stay where you be an' play ring-o'-roses wi' the bairns,' he grinned, 'and keep yer nose out of what don't concern ye!'

Damn them then!

Patrick wrenched himself free of the chanting prancing urchins. They could batter each other to death for all he cared. Grimly, he hoped they would.

He spung round angrily and almost knocked Sarah Rigby to the ground.

Purposefully she walked up to the belligerent doorkeeper, pushing him aside with a sweep of her arm.

'Out of my way, Knocker White,' she demanded, her voice dangerously low, 'and get those children out of the alley before they get hurt!'

'Yes, miss!'

Obediently the man stepped aside to admit her then

the familiar fist shot out again and Patrick found his way blocked once more.

'This feller says he's a doctor, Miss Sarah.'

'That's right — let him in,' Sarah commanded. 'He's with me.'

The man stood aside.

'Sorry, me old mucker!'

He grinned sheepishly.

'Got to be careful, ye' see — there's some funny folks about, these days . . .'

Patrick ducked his head and entered the tap-room, an unaccustomed hurt pulsing inside him.

They hadn't wanted him! He had been reared in Lace Street but he wasn't one of them any more. He'd seen more street fights than Knocker White had had hot dinners, he thought grimly, yet for two pins they'd have spat in his face and sent him on his way again.

They were his own people and they didn't own him! It had needed the quiet authority of a slip of a woman they knew and trusted to provide his passport into the Compass tavern in Leather Lane.

He blinked his eyes through the haze of choking paraffin smoke. His breath hissed sharply between his teeth as he became aware of the devastation within and, pain and anger forgotten, he groped his way across the room to where Sarah stood.

If only he were not so very tired and confused . . .

The Irish immigrants had scrambled thankfully on deck to take their first look at Liverpool. They had blessed themselves and thanked the Almighty and Saint Christopher for a safe passage and for the tall beacon on

Everton Heights that beckoned them into the safety of the river.

But those who stood at the ship's rail were the lucky ones for there were many among their number who were ill and vomiting and none of the *Cornucopia's* passengers had been sorry to leave the creaking wooden ship and set their feet on dry land again.

Most of them had sailed from Dublin to Dumfries then south to Liverpool, spending three days and nights herded into the ship's hold, tight-packed and little better than ballast.

The *Cornucopia* had ridden low in the water and the voyage had not been a comfortable one. Those who were not ill stretched their cramped limbs thankfully. Some made off quickly to find relatives with whom they might stay; others lingered by the quayside, uncertain and apprehensive.

Already most of the crew had disappeared into the tangle of dockside alleys before their womenfolk could catch up with them and their pay, each man in search of his own particular delight.

But those who were ill cared little for anything save that they had arrived at last and it was those sick who found their way to the house in Abercromby Square and patiently waited for the help they had been told would not be refused.

'It's a long time ye'll be sitting there,' Molly O'Keefe told them, 'for the doctor is away to a fight and heaven only knows when he'll be back to see to ye!'

But they waited for all that because there was nothing else for them to do and nowhere for them to go.

'Sir, I sent the patients away,' Molly protested hotly to Adam, 'but a fresh lot has just come and and they'll not budge. Just sitting there they are, staring at nothing and saying nothing. Strangers they are to me. I'm thinking they're new in from the old country, God help the poor creatures,' she sighed.

'I'll get up, Molly, and see what I can do,' Adam tried to reassure her. 'They may only be trying to find a bed for the night and think that perhaps they can get one here.'

'Well they can't and that's for sure, Doctor Adam. Glory be, we're bustin' at the seams already!'

'I know, Molly, I know,' Adam smiled gently, 'but if there are any sick amongst them, perhaps I can help. I must not stay in bed any longer. Already Sarah and Patrick are strained to the utmost. At least I can attend to the sick.'

And not all Molly's pleading had been able to deter Adam Carmichael as unsteadily he walked down the stairs.

The sick from the *Cornucopia*, when he saw them, complained to Adam of stomach pains and vomiting and there seemed little that he could do for them but administer a dose of mixture.

Conditions on the immigrant ships were near intolerable, he knew. In all probability the sickness would clear up when they had adjusted to dry land again.

He was relieved when the last of them left for he had not thought he could become so weak and the exertion of leaving his bed had brought on spasms of coughing once more.

'Is that them all gone then, Doctor?'

Molly set bread and a bowl of soup on Adam's desk. 'Now drink it all up and then be back to bed with ye. What Miss Sarah is going to say when she gets back, I'd not like to think about!'

Adam smiled his thanks.

'Do you think we need to mention it to Sarah?'

'Maybe not, doctor, for won't herself be sure to find out anyway? 'Tis no use telling lies,' she sighed. 'So drink up your broth, doctor darling, and be away to your bed again,' she urged, ''tis yourself that's in need of a physician, and that's for sure . . .'

Patrick Norris coughed in the choking fumes that hung heavy on the air in the Compass tavern. The oil lamp had been knocked over in the brawl and the rug that had been hastily thrown over it still smouldered and smoked.

'Open the window,' Patrick commanded the man at the door who seemed now to have accepted the stranger in their midst, 'and don't let anyone in here!'

But there was little fear of further intrusion. The men who fought in the alley would continue their sport until the children who kept watch at either end of the narrow way yelled 'Peelers!'

But the constable and his assistant – wise men both – would not appear until the rabble had all but exhausted themselves. Those worthy upholders of law and order knew better than risk a cracked head for a mob to whom a street brawl, from whatever cause it had started, was as good as a cock-fight.

Now the small, low-hung room contained only frightened women, some of them crying softly, some of them sitting quietly, stupefied by cheap gin.

The landlord set down candles and nodded towards the corner of the room.

'She's the only one that's hurt real bad,' he said. 'Best see what you can do for she's bleeding something 'orrible.'

A young girl lay on the floor, eyes closed tightly in a paper-white face.

She had been viciously slashed by a bottle or a knife and her injured arm lay awkwardly by her side.

'Quick!' Patrick demanded. 'A tourniquet!'

Deftly Sarah cut a length of bandage, knotting the ends with efficient, steady fingers. She handed it to Patrick with a small piece of wood the size of a lead pencil.

Expertly Patrick twisted the piece of cloth until it bit into the soft flesh of the injured limb.

'Now hold up her arm.'

Sarah took the blood-stained hand, looking down as she did into the bruised and shattered face of the girl.

Patrick wrung out a cloth in a bowl of water, gently cleaning away the marks of brutality.

'Who could do such a thing? She's little more than a child!'

He turned accusingly to the landlord.

'Why did you let her in?'

'Let her in? Lord luv ye, doctor, I can't keep 'em out! And anyway, they're good for trade. If they didn't tout here they'd do it somewhere else.'

'You mean this girl is on the streets?'

'Aye, sir.'

Patrick closed his eyes in disgust. At least, he thought, there appeared to be little damage to her face that time would not heal.

'It's only her arm,' Patrick turned to Sarah, 'but she's lost a great deal of blood and I'll have to stitch. Who is she, do you know?'

Sarah nodded, her face grave.

'She's Kate Tarleton. She comes of respectable folks but all her family died in the '47 epidemic. I suppose she looked after herself the only way she knew how.'

'I see,' Patrick nodded grimly.

His revulsion and disgust were not directed at the poor scrap who lay hurt and bleeding at his feet but at a society that allowed such circumstances to exist.

'There were these seamen came in from the *Cornucopia*, sir,' the landlord explained, anxiously. 'Kate Tarleton had dealings with one of them then there was trouble over money. Well, you know how one thing leads to another? Afore you could say "Wet Nelly" they'd wrecked the place!'

The *Cornucopia*!

Sarah tried to blot the name from her mind. There was the devil's thumb-print on that packet. She brought ill-luck with her every time she sailed into the Mersey.

Cornucopia. Jonah-ship. A packet that had once borne another name.

Sarah heard Dicky-Sam's voice at the doorway. Somehow it helped to pull her thoughts back to reality.

'Hullo, fairy!' chirped the little man as he gazed aloft at Knocker White's great hairy frame. 'You got Miss Sarah and Doctor Norris in there, then?'

'Here we are, Dicky-Sam,' Sarah called. 'Try to get a cab will you? Ask the driver to wait at the bottom of the alley.'

She turned to Patrick.

'We'll have to take Kate home with us,' she said.

'But Sarah, we can't. There's no room!' Patrick protested.

'There'll be room tomorrow. There's one due to leave the ward in the morning.'

Patrick saw the grim set of Sarah's lips. It would be useless to argue with her, he knew.

'We'll manage until then,' she asserted.

She would find a mattress, somewhere. They'd manage.

They always did and anyway she vowed, here was one poor creature who wasn't going back on the streets! If it meant her sleeping on the floor, Sarah asserted silently, Kate Tarleton was going back to *The Haven*.

Sarah smiled as the young girl's eyes flickered open.

'Hullo, Kate,' she said gently. 'Do you know who I am?'

'Aye, miss.'

The soft brown eyes brimmed over with tears.

'You'll not let the constable take me, miss? I'm not bad,' she whispered; 'not real bad. I wouldn't have started on the game if I could've got respectable work.'

'I know, child, I know.'

Sarah took the small thin hand in hers as the injured girl cried out in sudden pain.

'Hold on tight, Kate. The doctor won't be long, now.'

Patrick tied and snipped the last stich then smiled encouragement at Kate Tarleton. Not so very long ago he might not have shown such tolerance towards a street-woman but now he was remembering Aunt Hetty. Perhaps, thought Patrick, if he'd cared a little more his aunt might not be lying sick at *The Haven*.

Maybe, if someone had cared a little about Kate Tarleton, she might not be lying on the floor of the Compass tavern, a woman of the world before she had scarcely had time to be a child.

Sarah was right, thought Patrick. They would have to take Kate back to *The Haven*. She was a pretty child and fair game for the madams who provided young girls for lecherous old men. They would manage, he supposed.

Gently he helped the girl to her feet.

'Come along, little Kate,' he whispered, carefully gathering her into his arms. 'You're coming home with us.'

Sarah lifted her head then smiled tremulously into Patrick's eyes.

In that wordless moment of complete understanding he knew that however awful the day had been, however sickening and frustrating, Sarah's smile had made it all worth while.

Patrick lowered his body into the chair by Adam's bedside feeling that he would never again find the strength to leave it.

'You look utterly beaten, Patrick.'

Grave concern showed on Adam's face. 'Oh, I blame myself. I had no right to lay here while you and Sarah worked yourselves to a standstill.'

Patrick forced a grin to his lips.

'But you've been doing it for years, Adam, and anyway, it was only a fight that started over a prostitute. We brought her back with us. Sarah is settling her down, now.'

The door opened and Molly beamed her way into the room with a tray of tea and thick slices of bread and dripping.

'You'll be needing this I'm thinking, doctor!'

Gratefully Patrick accepted the mug of tea.

'Molly O'Keefe, 'tis an angel ye are!' he smiled.

'Now, there's no need for levity, sir, if you'll pardon me, for it's awful news I've heard from the lamplighter.'

'Bad news?' Patrick enquired, lazily, knowing that whatever it was he was fast learning to take one blow after another.

'Aye, Doctor Patrick. The *Cornucopia* docked on the late tide. There were sick aboard – a lot of them. They say it's the fever. They've brought more cholera into the port.'

Adam's face blanched.

'Is that true, Molly? Are you *sure* it's true?'

'Sure I'm sure,' Molly replied, bitterly, 'and some of the sick here at evening surgery as you well know, sir.'

Patrick felt his stomach do a somersault.

'You took a surgery this evening, Adam?'

Adam nodded reluctantly.

'And were there passengers here from the *Cornucopia*?'

'One or two, perhaps.'

'What were their symptoms?' Patrick demanded. 'Were any of them infected?'

'I think not,' Adam said quietly, willing his voice to be steady. 'I know cholera better than most, Patrick.'

But Adam's heart was thumping uncomfortably. He should have realized, he thought. He, above all, should have known. But he had been so tired; so very tired.

'It will be all right,' he said, softly.

But he was looking at his trembling fingers. Molly had brought him bread and broth when surgery had finished, and he had eaten it without thinking.

He, who should have known better, had not first washed his hands!

He clenched his hands tightly.

'Let it not be true?' he prayed, silently.

But how could he be sure? The symptoms of the *Cornucopia* passengers he had attended might well have been the result of the close-confining of bodies in an airless, crowded hold but they could have foretold something far more sinister.

With a gesture of near-despair Adam ran his fingers through his hair and felt the clammy sweat of fear on his forehead.

Gently Patrick's fingertips touched the pulse at Adam's wrist.

'You are more tired than you will admit. You should not have left your bed. Perhaps now,' he added gravely, 'you will listen to your doctor's advice!'

Adam reached for the comfort of his friend's hand, clasping it tightly with slender, anxious fingers.

'Patrick,' he whispered, 'I didn't want to ask this when Molly was in the room, but could I have been wrong? The symptoms of the sick from the *Cornucopia* – could they have been . . .?'

His voice trailed uneasily away and the dread question was left unspoken.

Patrick's hand tightened reassuringly round Adam's.

'Were you wrong, do you think?'

'I don't know.' Adam's voice betrayed a tremble of fear. 'God help me, I don't know!'

'Then tell me,' Patrick asked gently, 'if Molly hadn't told you that more cholera had come into the port, would you now be doubting your own diagnosis?'

'No,' Adam hesitated. 'No, I don't think I would.'

Patrick rose to his feet.

'Then let's leave it for tonight – sleep on it. We are both tired. Tomorrow it will all seem different, you'll see.'

Patrick smiled down into the pale face, realizing afresh how ill his friend was.

'You are right, Patrick. We are all tired and tomorrow is another day,' Adam smiled gently back. 'I think I would like to sleep, now.'

Patrick picked up the candlestick.

'Then I will wish you goodnight.'

A little of the tension left Adam's face and he lay back on his pillows.

'Goodnight, Patrick, and God bless you for all you are doing for us.'

Patrick nodded his head and then turning abruptly on his heel walked quickly away. He had wanted to find words that would give comfort but suddenly he found he was unable to meet Adam's eyes. It was something he could not explain. He only knew that for an instant he had known a feeling of awful foreboding.

Was it the fault of the flickering candleflame and the long, dark shadows it cast? Perhaps animal fear tingled its way down his spine because he was tired and hot and the smell of the tavern in Leather Lane was still foul in his nostrils.

He shook his head as if to clear it of such morbid thoughts. He was being foolish, afraid that if things got any worse he could no longer cope with the situation. A man felt like that, Patrick reasoned, when every nerve in his body screamed out for sleep.

Wearily he walked towards Hetty Norris's room and gently pushed open the door. He was almost relieved when her gentle breathing told him she was sleeping soundly.

Sarah blinked open her eyes in the unfamiliar room then realized she had spent what was left of the night in the small hot attic. Already the early morning sun was pouring through the fanlight in the ceiling and she knew that today would be no different from the other sultry days that had plagued the town for weeks on end.

She pulled her knees up to her chin and sat for a little while with her arms clasped round them, willing herself to leave her bed, uncomfortable though it was.

Across the room Kate Tarleton slept uneasily, her injured arm lying lightly splinted and awkward on the bed at her side. Her face showed the marks of the previous night's horror in angry bruises and lips that were swollen and distorted.

At least thought Sarah, the girl had youth on her side. Given care, her injuries would leave no scars. But the other kind of wounding, the degradation of the life she had been forced to lead; the loneliness she had known since her family died and the harshness of the world into which she had been thrust, might never heal and could only be eased by time and love.

Sarah lowered her feet to the bare floor, groping with her toes for her slippers.

Quietly and quickly she dressed then walked carefully from the room.

On the half-landing below she paused, remembering that last night she had not called in to see Adam before creeping thankfully into her attic bed.

Now, as she walked into his room, she knew at once that something was wrong.

'What is it?'

Instantly she was at his side.

'Adam, you are not well! Let me call Patrick?'

'No, Sarah.'

Adam shaped his lips into a small smile of reassurance. 'It is all right. I did not sleep, that is all.'

'But you should have asked Patrick for a draught.'

'I did and he gave me one. It didn't work.'

'Why not, Adam? What is worrying you?'

Adam's soft brown eyes clouded over. Anxiously his fingers plucked at the counterpane.

'Tell me about it,' Sarah urged, sensing that something inside him was crying out for help.

For a moment he lay quietly, his eyes closed, a small nerve flicking at the corner of his mouth. Then, as though it were an effort to say it he whispered, 'I think I was wrong about the *Cornucopia* patients. I diagnosed mal-de-mer when I should have known it was cholera.'

Sarah frowned. *The Cornucopia patients?*

Adam saw the doubt on her face.

'Have you spoken with Molly since last night?'

'No,' Sarah shook her head. 'I was on my way downstairs to the kitchen when I decided to look into your room.'

'Then you can't know. Last night, when you and Patrick were at the tavern in Leather Lane, some patients came to *The Haven*. Molly couldn't get them to leave so I attended to them. They were from the *Cornucopia*, Sarah. I thought they were only suffering from a bad dose of sea-sickness — at least until Molly told us there was the fever on the *Cornucopia* — cholera.'

Sarah's mouth went dry.

'And now,' she prompted, her suddenly-stiff lips forcing out the words, 'you think it wasn't sea-sickness? You think it could have been — something else?'

'I *know* it was, Sarah. The stomach cramps, high temperatures and sickness. I should have known!'

'Perhaps you were wrong?'

Adam turned his head and gazed into Sarah's eyes shaking his head wordlessly.

'Tell me what is to be done, Adam.'

The smell of fear was real in Sarah's nostrils but it was not for herself.

Adam had been in contact with cholera and already he was sick and weak.

'Tell me, and I will do as you say.'

Adam was grateful that Sarah did not assail his ears with easy words of comfort.

'First, I must talk to Patrick again. Last night, I thought

I had not made the wrong diagnosis. Now, when I have lain awake thinking about it, I am certain the *Cornucopia* patients who came here had cholera. I must do what I can to contain it within *The Haven* and if the worst doesn't happen then so much the better. But first it must be reported to Doctor Duncan.'

Sarah nodded. 'And then?'

'I must be isolated, Sarah. My food must be left at the door and no one here must come near me.'

'That is nonsense, Adam!' Sarah gasped. 'Do you really think I would agree to that?'

'It is the most sensible thing to do, Sarah, until we are sure I am not infected.'

'How long . . .?'

'Three days,' Adam shrugged. 'Perhaps less.'

There was a tremble in his voice.

'But is that absolutely necessary, Adam?'

'I think it is. A great many people come to this house. If we at *The Haven* got ill, how would the work continue? There would be no one to attend the sick. Think how many people would suffer.'

Other people, thought Sarah. It is always other people Adam thinks about.

'Couldn't you go to your family in Scotland, Adam? You would get rest and good food there and the country air would help your cough as well. I have asked this of you many times in the past. Will you not go, now?'

Adam shook his head.

'Once, Sarah, it might have been possible. Now, knowing what I do, I couldn't be responsible for spreading the infection and that is surely what I would be doing by going home.'

'But we are not sure there is any danger. We are not

even sure the *Cornucopia* passengers who came here were suffering from it, are we?'

She lifted her eyes to his, imploring him to tell her she could be right, but Adam shook his head.

'It is almost certain I am a cholera contact, Sarah,' he replied sadly.

'Then you shall not shut yourself away, at least not from me. I have nursed the fever before and I shall nurse it again, if needs be!'

With a sob in her voice she reached out and drew Adam's head towards her, resting her cheek on his hair.

'I will look after you, Adam,' she whispered. 'Do you think I could let you be alone at such a time? I will take care of you.'

Her voice broke huskily and her arms tightened round Adam's too-thin shoulders.

'I shall never leave you but it will all come right, Adam. I promise you *it will be all right*.'

Deliberately she emphasised each word, willing all the strength in her young body into his.

Desperately Adam clung to her. He was grateful for the comfort of her nearness for he felt utterly alone and very afraid. He must not be ill for there was too much still to be done; so many people who needed his help. If he were to die, who would be left to care about them but Sarah?

'Are you sure? Do you really believe it will be all right, Sarah?'

'I truly believe it, my dear,' she whispered, tenderly.

It was thus that Patrick found them. They had not heard his approach for he had walked quietly lest Adam should still be sleeping.

For a moment Patrick stood unmoving, almost unable to believe what he saw only too plainly. Then, scarcely breathing lest a creaking floorboard should betray his presence, he edged his way carefully back again down the long narrow passageway.

The sight of so tender a scene disturbed him and he was at a loss to understand why. He and Adam were friends of long-standing. They had talked intimately in the past of girls they had kissed and girls they had courted. Why then did the sight of Adam and Sarah in so loving an embrace make his body shake almost uncontrollably? It should have been obvious to him, he thought as he walked carefully back in the direction of Hetty Norris's room, that Sarah and Adam must be in love. Why else would a woman live and work in the conditions that existed at *The Haven*? Women would endure anything for the sake of the man they loved. Women were wondrous queer cattle!

Adam must find Sarah very easy to love. There was a quiet strength about her, a unique aura of gentleness that seemed to wrap her round wherever she went and whatever she was doing. And Sarah Rigby was beautiful, Patrick conceded. He had not realized it until last night when suddenly in the garden he had been only too well aware of it. He had felt an inexplicable peace in the gathering dusk with the evening scent of flowers around them.

Patrick jerked his thoughts back to reality. He was being foolish. He was making a fuss about nothing. He was betrothed to Arabella Harrington and Sarah and Adam were in love. It was as simple as that.

Purposefully, he knocked on the door of his aunt's bedroom.

Seven

Hetty Norris struggled into a sitting position and announced that it was time for her to return to Lace Street.

That she looked so much better was a profound relief to Patrick but he had no intention, yet, of letting her go back to her lonely house.

'You will do no such thing, Aunt,' he retorted firmly. 'You still need rest and a lot more of Molly's cooking.'

The little woman nodded her head in agreement.

'I will admit, boy, that I am tempted to stay a while but there are things I must do.'

'Like scrubbing floors and taking in washing?' Patrick asked bluntly.

Hetty Norris bit her lip.

She needed her work. To stay longer at *The Haven*, pleasant though it was, might mean the loss of her regular customers and that she could not allow to happen.

There was Rebecca Solomon to be paid, too, and Black Becky's clients knew full well that once they allowed themselves to fall behind with their payments they and the little they owned would be at the mercy of the tallyman.

'I would like to be where you are, Patrick. I see so little of you now and being waited on has been a rare treat. But I must go.'

'Why, Aunt? What excuse can there be for ignoring my advice?'

'Excuse, you young puppy! Since when did Hetty Norris need an excuse for anything she did?'

Patrick smiled. Aunt Hetty was indeed getting better.

'You may rant as much as you like, Aunt, but I shall tell Miss Rigby to hide your boots. See how far you get then!'

Hetty Norris conceded defeat.

'Now there,' she said, adroitly changing the subject, 'is a fine young woman for you. There's a real lady and no mistake.'

'Why do you say that? Do you know who she is?'

'No, Patrick, I don't but I know good breeding when I see it. I worked for gentlefolk for long enough.'

And who, wondered Patrick, had those gentlefolk been?

Tantalising memories of a large house came flooding back once more.

Were Aunt Hetty's gentlefolk his own kin?

'Who were they, Aunt?'

'Oh, fine folks who once lived in St Anne Street. They were good people and they treated their servants well.'

'Did they have a daughter?'

'Of course they had a daughter, boy. They had three daughters. What a question to ask!'

'Which house was it – what number . . .?'

Hetty Norris glanced sideways at Patrick.

The young whippersnapper was up to his questioning again. Some day, she decided, she would tell him. One day, he would have to be told; one day – when the time was right . . .

'Which number? I don't remember!' she flung back irritably. 'It was a long time ago; more than twenty years back. My memory isn't what it was. I can't carry numbers in my head!'

There was a knock on the door and old Hetty had reason to be grateful for Molly O'Keefe's timely interruption.

'Well then, it's better you're looking this morning, Miss Norris,' she beamed. 'And here's meself with some porridge and a nice plate of thin bread and butter.'

She arranged her plenteous hips on the bedside chair and settled down for a chat.

'See that she eats it all up, Molly,' called Patrick as he closed the door behind him.

Weak though she was he mused as he walked down the wide, bare staircase, Aunt Hetty was cunning as ever. It would take more than near-starvation to dull those keen old wits.

But he must find out who his real family were. Somehow he must make Aunt Hetty understand how important it was to him and to Arabella.

Arabella, his mind echoed. By now he should have joined her in Harrogate yet he hadn't even been able to find the time to write her a letter and beg her understanding.

He shrugged his shoulders moodily. Find time for letterwriting in Abercromby Square?

But today at all costs he must make the time to pay a visit to Hanover Street and one of the few of Adam's patients who could still afford to pay for treatment. And he could, whilst he was in the vicinity, pay Rebecca Solomon a visit for the old money-lender lived in nearby Paradise Street. Sooner or later Patrick knew, he would have to get to the bottom of the mystery of the tallyman's calls at Lace Street.

He sighed. It was something he wasn't looking forward to doing but it had to be done and who knew but that it might, perhaps, have some oblique connection with the *Private Matter*?

Rebecca Solomon, for all her undoubted wealth, lived in a small house at the meaner end of Paradise Street.

Carefully Patrick picked his way amongst men and women who lolled in small silent huddles in the hot July sun and tried to avoid the curious glances and satisfied smirks showing plainly their pleasure that yet another young buck seemed forced to seek the benefit of Becky's money-bags.

Patrick rapped on the shabby door with the head of his cane, outwardly affecting a confidence he was far from feeling.

'Come in. Come in, do!'

The room in which Rebecca Solomon sat was stiflingly hot and made the more so by a large fire that burned in the grate.

'Shut the door!' the old woman grumbled, hunching her shawl more closely round her shoulders. 'Can't abide draughts.'

Patrick looked round the cluttered room with distaste.

The thick carpet that covered the entire floor was almost hidden by rich rugs and everywhere was evidence of the money-lender's squirrel-like mentality.

Ornaments covered the dresser and table and too many chairs, footstools and cupboards made it almost impossible to walk across the room in comfort.

'Well now, my dear, what can Rebecca do for you?' she croaked. 'Been playing cards? Got a little wench into trouble, maybe? Been a naughty boy, have you?'

With dignity Patrick removed his hat and gloves and laid them carefully on the edge of the table.

'I am Doctor Patrick Norris, ma'am,' he returned, stiffly.

'Oh?'

Clearly Rebecca Solomon was not impressed. She had

no need to be. She was rich beyond the dreams of most men and all else paled into insignificance beside that fact.

Patrick shuffled his feet.

'Sit down, my dear. Sit down, do,' Black Becky jabbed a wizened finger at the chair opposite, 'and tell me what I can do for you.'

'Ma'am, I will come straight to the point. How much money does Miss Hester Norris of Lace Street owe you?'

'That's a private matter between me and Hetty Norris!'

'Then now, madam, it is private no longer,' Patrick returned in his best London manner, 'and I will be obliged if you will answer my question.'

'She borrowed eighty pounds.'

'Eighty pounds!' *A small fortune!* 'When?'

'Oh seven, maybe eight years gone.'

'And how much does she give you each week?'

'Three shillings and sixpence.'

Patrick took his purse from his pocket.

'I would like to pay off what is owing.'

'And what if you can't, young sir? What if I'm content with things the way they are?'

'What do you mean by that?'

'Hetty Norris is a good payer – no trouble at all.' The black eyes narrowed. 'Maybe that's the way I like it.'

'Then I am sorry, Mrs Solomon, but I must insist. How much?'

'Thirty-five pounds.'

The reply was prompt and precise; the eyes that met Patrick's did not waver.

'*Thirty-five pounds?* But that is ridiculous! Why, the debt must have almost been paid, by now!'

'Ah, the loan perhaps, but what about the interest? What about compensation for the risk involved? What about the upkeep of me tallyman? Eighty sovereigns is a lot of money to lend a washerwoman! What about a little extra, eh, for me kindness and trust?'

Anger darted in bright red flashes before Patrick's eyes.

'You are a cheat and a trickster! You're a . . . you're a greedy old bitch!' Patrick spat, all pretence at gentility abandoned.

'Now then, young man, wait on! I miscalculated. It's thirty-seven pounds, now, for your impudence! And whilst we're about it, there was no one in at Lace Street when my gentleman called yesterday. Hopped it, has she?'

White-hot with seething rage Patrick spilled the contents of his purse into his hand then slowly counted out the money, slamming it onto the table.

'There you are,' he jerked, his words almost choking him. 'There's thirty pounds and you can take it or leave it! And I'll have a receipt, too, for the clearance of the debt!'

Rebecca Solomon pondered a while, then realizing the gentleman she thought might be easy-meat was hard as flint beneath the fine clothes, she reached for a quill.

'No justice, there ain't. Taking advantage of an old woman, it is,' she grumbled as she scratched pen to paper.

Patrick read the receipt carefully then folded it and placed it in his pocket.

The money he had paid Rebecca Solomon was almost all he possessed. Now he would be entering that most solemn state of matrimony with little more than ten pounds to his name.

'Now listen to me, you miserable old crow,' he spat. 'If your tallyman bothers Miss Norris again, I swear I'll break his miserable neck – in five places!'

Slamming the door behind him he walked back towards *The Haven*.

What had prompted him ever to return to Liverpool only God in His wisdom knew, but of one thing Patrick Norris was certain. The sooner he got himself out of it, the better!

Silently fuming he walked towards the Haymarket and the Folly Fair where farmers from the countryside around gathered to sell their produce and where, if they could afford it, housewives brought milks and eggs, cheese and butter.

Today, the fair was ill-attended. Farmers were loath to visit the town where it was known the fever was spreading with alarming rapidity.

But Patrick hardly noticed; he strode on blindly into Pembroke Place, remembering with a downward quirk of his mouth the old infirmary where once he and Adam had spent so many weary hours in the early years of their apprenticeship.

It had mattered then that those who entered such a place had little hope of leaving it alive. It had grieved him that infirmaries were places where a poor wretch was consigned to die with as much dignity as he could muster. In the small cold hours of the morning when most souls take leave of their earthly bodies, he and Adam had argued and debated and would have changed the world if they could, such had been the passion of their youth.

But London had beckoned to Patrick; only Adam had been true to himself. Adam had stayed in the mean streets and for his reward he had lungs that were choked with consumption and a heart heavy with fear because a sailing packet had brought more cholera into the port.

Angry with life though he still was, a small voice of conscience whispered in Patrick's ear that men and women would be waiting patiently at *The Haven* for surgery to commence and that Sarah would not be able to manage alone.

Crossing the road he walked quickly past the fever hospital, the oakum sheds, the workhouse and the lunatic asylum.

What a terrible collection of misery that street contained thought Patrick as he turned his back on Brownlow Hill and its macabre collection of buildings that stood high above the town and struck fear into the hearts of the poor.

Those were the places wherein hope finally died; but then – what hope was there for anyone in the festering port of Liverpool except for those who had the luck to land the means to get out of it?

As he walked up the steps to the open front door of *The Haven*, the resentment caused by the injustice of life in general and Rebecca Solomon in particular still throbbed inside him like an aching tooth. Perhaps it was because of this that when Sarah's anxious eyes told him silently that something was amiss, he gave an exclamation of annoyance.

'What is it *now*?' he asked brusquely, biting off each word as he fought to control the mixture of despair and anger that slapped a warning at the pit of his stomach.

Then, instantly contrite at the sight of her stricken face he asked more gently, 'Is something wrong?'

Sarah nodded and beckoned with her head for Patrick to follow her to the ward.

'It's the Hanson baby,' she whispered.

'Little Ben? But he's the only one in the ward who *isn't* sick.'

'I know, Patrick; I know.'

She had no time for explanations.

'Then what is it?'

As far as Patrick was concerned when last he visited the ward, the Hanson baby had been in perfect health, apart perhaps from the eye-teeth he was cutting. It had been his young parents, Tilly and George, who had been brought to *The Haven* with extensive burns when a fire had blazed their little home into a heartbreaking rubble.

Now they were well enough to leave and would have done so already had they been able to find some corner of a cheap lodging-house or empty cellar to live in. It was only Sarah's compassion, Patrick knew, that had kept the Hanson family at *The Haven*, for so long.

Sarah stirred the jug she carried.

'What is that?' Patrick asked, peeling off his coat.

'An emetic.'

'Salt and warm water?'

'Yes. I've got to make Ben vomit. It's our only hope.'

'What has he swallowed?'

'Laudanum.' Sarah's reply was terse.

'*Laudanum?* For God's sake, *how*?'

Patrick received no answer but he hadn't expected one, for a glance at the child who lolled like a rag doll in his mother's arms told him that time was precious.

'Bring him to the window and slap his face,' Sarah commanded Tilly Hanson, willing her voice to be steady.

'Do anything, but for pity's sake, don't let him go to sleep?'

'I'm trying, miss, but he keeps dropping off,' the young mother sobbed. 'He isn't going to die is he?'

'No, ma'am,' Patrick interjected, expertly forcing open the little jaws with his fingers, 'but you must help us. Ben must be made to drink all this salt and water. If we can make him sick, he'll be all right. Do you understand?'

Tilly Hanson nodded, her eyes dilated with fear. Beside

her, pale and anxious, stood her husband and in the corner Dicky-Sam sat unspeaking, his face white as chalk. There was no word from the other patients in the ward, merely a silent sympathy as they watched the water being forced into the mouth of the feebly protesting child.

'How much laudanum did he take?'

Patrick addressed Sarah but his eyes did not leave the child for an instant.

'A spoonful. A large spoonful.'

'A *what*?' Patrick exploded, doubling his efforts with frantic haste.

He turned to the child's father.

'Hold his nose. Make him gulp down air as he swallows. *He's got to be sick!*'

There was no anger in Patrick and this Sarah recognized. She was grateful for his presence. She had never been so glad to see anyone in the whole of her life as she had been when Patrick returned from his sick-visiting.

Now Patrick was icy-cold, working efficiently and without emotion but when the danger was over – if ever it *was* over – Sarah knew that the devil would have to be paid for what was happening.

For a few moments that stretched away into an eternity, it seemed that they were making no progress. Then, with a protesting cry from little Ben and a gasp of relief from Patrick, they knew that the danger was over.

'Good,' Patrick whispered, grimly. 'Now, if we can keep him awake for a few hours longer, I think he'll do.'

He turned to Sarah.

'Will you arrange to have this mess cleared up?' he demanded brusquely, nodding towards the floor and hating himself for what he was asking. He knew Sarah would have to clean the floor herself but he was still hurting inside.

It hadn't just been the finding of Adam in Sarah's arms or Rebecca Solomon's avarice; it was the happenings of the previous four days that he could still scarcely believe. The overdose of laudanum had only set the seal on his anger. He wondered how Adam – and Sarah, too – could endure to work at *The Haven* day after day, for years.

But that, he decided, was their business. Just as soon as he could he would be out of the place. He would be back with Arabella and Doctor Harrington and in the dignity and sanity of the Harley Street practice, he would be able to forget Liverpool entirely.

Patrick straightened his shoulders. First though, there were things to be done. Sarah must be told in no uncertain words that the dispensing of laudanum or any other such drug was not undertaken by meddling amateurs. What Adam permitted was between himself and his professional conscience but since he, Patrick Norris, had assumed responsiblity for *The Haven*, albeit for only a few days, it was his duty to see that she understood the enormity of her mistake.

Perhaps, he thought reluctantly, what he really wanted to do was to convince himself that Sarah didn't matter to him; that the unmistakably loving embrace he had seen hadn't stabbed into him like a knife. He wanted to believe it didn't matter, but that was not true. He knew that Sarah Rigby disturbed him deeply. He knew that if he let himself, he could love her and be in love with her. What he could feel for Sarah was not acknowledged in genteel society. It was the earthy love of a man for his mate; the kind of love that would want to make him defend her with his life. What he felt for Sarah was not part of a contracted, discreetly arranged match that would provide heirs with nicety. He wanted Sarah's lithe young body in his arms, with her hair tumbling the pillow. He wanted her to bear his children . . .

'Damn! Damn! Damn!' he swore, shaking his head as if to deny his thoughts.

He heard the clanking of a bucket and knew Sarah had finished her menial task of cleaning up the ward floor.

'Madam!' he yelled, the shame he felt for his surging thoughts finding release, 'Will you be kind enough to step in here?'

It was more a command than a request.

Patrick opened the dispensary door, deliberately walking through it ahead of Sarah. He closed it firmly then turned to face her.

She was drying her hands on her apron and he saw they were rough and cracked from scrubbing and washing. He wanted to take them gently into his and hold them to his cheek.

He said instead, 'Do you appreciate the seriousness of this morning's happenings, ma'am?'

Sarah nodded, her eyes still downcast.

'And are you in the habit of dispensing drugs?'

'Yes – yes, I am.'

'Then I would have deemed it propitious if you had learned a little more about their dangers and a lot more about their dosage!'

Sarah looked up quickly, her eyes meeting his.

'Oh, but I do . . .'

She dropped her glance, again.

' . . I do know,' she faltered.

'Then tell me what it is? What is the correct dosage, ma'am, for an infant of eighteen months?'

'One drop, in water.'

Patrick reached for the bottle of brown liquid and held it dramatically on high.

'One drop, Miss Rigby, not one *spoonful*!'

'I know. Oh, truly I know, but you see, the baby was teething and fretful and I had twice before given him a sleeping draught. I'd had to think about the others in the ward, as well. Ben was disturbing their rest.'

'So, this time you thought you'd give him a little extra.'

There was no mistaking the sarcasm in Patrick's voice.

'Well, ma'am,' he continued when Sarah did not reply, 'whilst I am acting as Doctor Carmichael's locum you will not enter this dispensary or administer any dosage whatsoever without my express permission. Do you understand?'

Sarah nodded.

'Now, miss, you will give me the dispensary key.'

He thrust out his hand and silently she passed it to him then turned on her heel and went quickly from the room.

For a moment Patrick stood, the laudanum bottle still grasped in his hand.

Other women would have protested, he reasoned. They would have found excuses for their carelessness or used their feminine ways to escape the consequences of their actions. Arabella would have done it – indeed most women would have used similar tactics.

But not so Sarah Rigby. She had not coaxed or tried to lie. She had accepted words that ripped from him like poison-tipped darts without protest because she had been wrong.

How many other women would have done that, he asked himself dispassionately.

Quietly she had given him the key then left the room

without any display of dramatics. He wondered what she was doing now and knew that somewhere she would be crying quietly. He had seen the tears that ran silently down her cheeks for all she had done to hide them and as she turned her back on him and walked quickly from the room, it had taken all the strength in his body to stop himself from taking her in his arms and kissing away those tears.

He had made her suffer for his own frustrations and every word he had flung at her tore at his heart like a vicious pain.

'Oh, Sarah, my love,' he whispered to the empty little room.

Like an automaton Patrick dealt with the patients who had waited on the hard wooden benches in the entrance hall of *The Haven*. He remembered little of it save that there had been no one with fever symptoms. For this at least he was grateful for he knew that the outbreak had reached almost epidemic proportions and that it could only be a matter of time before it burst like some filthy growth and paralysed the town with its evil.

Almost as the last patient left there was a gentle tapping on the door and Patrick was glad that in all the turmoil at *The Haven*, one thing did not seem to change.

Always after surgery, Dicky-Sam brought in a mug of tea. It was as if he waited and timed it to the last second.

'Come in, Dicky,' called Patrick.

'Your tea, doctor. To be sure, I thought it would be dinner-time before you finished.'

'I was late in starting.'

'Yes, sir. I knows that and it's on that matter I have something to say.'

'About the Hanson baby, you mean?'

'Aye, sir. It was me as did it.'

'*You*, Dicky-Sam?'

Patrick almost shouted the words.

'Aye. There was nobody about, you see. You'd gone out and Miss Sarah was seeing to Doctor Adam, so I took it upon meself to help. Only I didn't help, did I, sir?'

'No, Dicky. You didn't help at all.'

Patrick took a long, deep breath, trying desperately to be calm. 'Do you usually give out medicines?'

'No, doctor, never. But the little lad hadn't slept all night on account of his teeth. They hadn't wanted to bother Miss Sarah last night, knowing she was took up with Kate Tarleton. So the poor little shaver bawled and cried all night and looked settled for crying all day, too.'

'And you thought you'd set up as a doctor and prescribe yourself? Was that it?'

'No, doctor, that wasn't it at all. Only they knew Miss Sarah had given little Ben a dose of the brown stuff before; Mrs Hanson showed me which bottle it was. I was trying to do something that would help Miss Sarah.'

'And instead you caused her a lot more trouble?'

'Aye, I did and I'll never go near that medicine room again, I swear it! I'm only good at seafaring and lifting things and I'm sticking to that, now.'

Patrick knew he should have been enraged. He should have dealt more sternly with the distraught little man but all passion, indeed, all feeling had drained from him. Sarah had been his whipping-boy. She had suffered the brunt of his ill-temper and suffered it for Dicky-Sam's mistake.

'Then remember that, Dicky,' Patrick said, almost wearily. 'Remember that today you nearly killed a child.'

'I'll never forget it, doctor.'

The unhappy old face bore witness to Dicky-Sam's sincerity.

'And now if you please, sir, I'll take me punishment.'

'Do you want to be punished?'

'No sir, but I aught to be.'

'Then I will punish you, Dicky-Sam. I will tell you something that will hurt you very much. Before surgery I accused Sarah of your mistake. I was rude to her; I said most ungentlemanly things to her; I shouted and I made her cry. And for all that, she took the blame herself. She let me believe she had given the overdose. She shielded *you!*'

'Lawks, sir, then you've punished me all right. You've given me better than a keel-hauling. I'd as leave give up me good leg as have Miss Sarah suffer. I loves and respects her too much to hurt her and God's my witness to that!'

Patrick looked with compassion at the distress of the weatherbeaten little seaman for he understood his feelings only too well.

Dicky-Sam loved Sarah, too. They both loved her, each in his different way and were bonded by it. Patrick knew Dicky-Sam's punishment could not have been more complete and he knew exactly how sad the cripple felt.

I hurt her too; not because I wanted to help her as Dicky did, he thought, almost sick with shame. I hurt her deliberately because I loved her almost unbearably. It is I who must take the blame.

'What can I do, Doctor Patrick, to make amends?'

'Nothing, Dicky – I'll do it. I'll make amends for both of us.'

Silently, his face contorted with misery, Dicky-Sam limped from the room.

*

Sarah was crossing the hall as Patrick opened the surgery door. For a moment they faced each other and he saw that her eyes were still moist from weeping. She said quietly, her voice husky with emotion, 'Do you want something?'

'Yes, Sarah. I want something very badly. I want your forgiveness. Will you give it to me, please?'

He said the words softly and humbly.

'How did you know?'

Sarah raised her eyes to his.

'That it was Dicky-Sam? He told me himself.'

'He was only trying to help. You weren't too hard on him, were you?'

'No, Sarah, I wasn't.'

No, my darling, his heart supplied, I vented my anger on you. I hurt you because I love you and because you belong to Adam . . .

He clenched his fists in an effort to stop himself reaching out for her.

'Then I'm grateful to you, Patrick. Dicky's a good little man. He tries so hard to help us.'

Her lip trembled and her voice betrayed the tears that were still very near the surface.

'Sarah, don't be upset. I am so ashamed of my behaviour that I don't know what to say or how to apologize enough.'

Sarah shook her head wordlessly, covering her face with her hands and Patrick knew she was crying again.

'Please, my dear,' he pleaded, 'don't cry.'

'I'm sorry, Patrick. Oh, I'm so sorry. I don't often cry but I get so tired, sometimes and it's all piling up . . .'

Of course it was all getting too much for her, Patrick agreed silently. It wasn't the work or the poverty – Sarah could have stood up to that; but now Adam was really ill and Sarah loved him.

Patrick saw that her shoulders were shaking silently. She looked so alone and defenceless that he held out his arms and felt a fierce joy when she came to them.

'There now,' he soothed. 'I understand. Let the tears come if it will help you.'

He laid his head on her hair and with a shock of delight imagined that the scent of honeysuckle still lingered there. Her body near his felt just as he knew it would feel and he wanted to hold her closer and gentle the hurt out of her. He wanted her lips beneath his; he wanted to see her eyes close with delight at his touch.

But she didn't love him. She could not know what feelings surged through him. *Sarah loved Adam.* Patrick knew he must say it again and again until it no longer had the power to hurt him.

Sarah loved Adam and he, Patrick Norris, could only give her his comfort and a shoulder to cry upon. That much he could do for her; that much, and no more.

Vaguely through his pulsing emotions Patrick heard the click of a door-latch and a swish of satin.

In his arms Sarah stiffened then pushed her hands against him in a small protest. He felt her turn in his arms, heard the sharp intake of her breath.

Reluctantly he raised his head and blinked rapidly then as the shifting haze resolved itself, he felt a cold slap of apprehension in the pit of his stomach.

Before him the figure outlined in the open doorway stood rigid as a statue.

He saw a face drained white in anger, blue eyes wide with shock, lips set tight in unspoken accusation.

For a moment he was hardly able to believe what he

saw. It seemed almost that the voice he heard was not his own as he gasped,

'Arabella!'

Eight

❖

'Arabella!' Patrick repeated, desperately willing his thoughts into some semblance of order.

He tried to hold out his arms in greeting but they hung like lead at his sides; he tried to step forward but his feet were incapable of movement.

He was not imagining it; Arabella was here, in Liverpool! She was wearing a blue travelling habit and tiny pink rosebuds nodded at the side of her bonnet. She was real yet now she was almost a stranger to him. She belonged in London, part of a life that now seemed so remote that it might never have happened.

Arabella was the woman he was soon to marry but she had no place in the house in Abercromby Square.

The quiet closing of a door told Patrick that Sarah had slipped away from them and it relieved a little of the tension inside him.

'I can't believe it,' he stammered. 'I had not expected . . .'

'No Patrick, it seems you had not!' Arabella whispered, each word a tight, sharp dart.

He heard the inward hiss of her breath and knew that soon the gates of shock and disbelief that held her would come crashing down before the torrent of her anger.

'But dearest,' he hastened, 'you misunderstand. What you saw –'

'What I *saw* Patrick seems to need no explanation!'

Patrick shrugged inwardly. He had been comforting Sarah – that at least was true – but the love he had felt, the wild upsurge of longing, the desire to never let her free from his arms were feelings he would never try to excuse.

But he could understand Arabella's anger for those feelings must have been mirrored only too plainly in his eyes.

'Sarah – Miss Rigby – was distressed,' he faltered. 'She and Adam are very close and Adam is ill.'

'I see.'

Arabella waited like a tightly-coiled spring for further explanation.

'You do not believe me,' Patrick accused, flailing blindly into the attack.

'I am finding it very hard!'

The reply was terse, each word bitten off sharply and spat out with venom.

'Look, Arabella, we can't talk here.'

Desperately Patrick played for time. Soon, if he were not careful, the full fury of Arabella's anger would release itself to be followed by tears and tantrums. He had witnessed such a scene before and he had no wish to see another. Nor had he, he thought grimly, the time or the patience to endure one.

He reached out for her arm.

'Come into the little parlour. It is cooler there, and quiet. We can talk – I can explain . . .'

But Arabella shook off his hand. Her body stiff with disapproval she reluctantly followed him. As he closed the door behind them she flung into the attack.

'A *few days*, Patrick! You said you would rejoin me within a few days. Almost a week went by without one word of explanation and I must come to *you*!'

Her eyes flashed like brittle glass and the paper-white cheeks now blazed red with uncontrolled temper.

'Things were not as I had expected to find them, Arabella, when I arrived here.'

'Nor, when *I* arrived, either!'

'You are determined to misunderstand. If you would listen to me, I could explain.'

'I do not doubt it for one instant, Patrick.'

'Arabella,' he appealed, his voice terse, 'I ask you to believe I am truly sorry.'

'Sorry? Sorry for what?' Her voice rose to near-hysteria. 'Are you sorry for what you have done or sorry I caught you doing it?'

Patrick let Arabella's anger wash over him. To protest further would only make a bad situation worse. She had, he acknowledged, cause for anger. If he were really truthful he must freely admit it. But at all costs, he must calm her.

Refusing to be drawn further, desperately trying to detach himself from her wrath, he stared grimly out of the window, seeing afresh the tangled garden that wilted now in the merciless shimmer of afternoon heat.

Could it have only been last night that Sarah sat there at his feet, her hair falling about her shoulders?

He jerked his thoughts back to the small sitting-room and waited for Arabella to continue to hurl her unhappiness at his back.

But his silence had the effect he desired. He heard a shuddering sob and a small sniff then waited as reluctant footsteps came slowly towards him.

She stood beside him, staring ahead. Presently, her voice stiff and dangerously quiet, she said, 'I want to go home to London. I want to go today, *now*, and I want you to come with me, Patrick.'

Had Arabella slapped his face she could not have startled Patrick more. He spun round to face her.

'I cannot,' he jerked. 'It is out of the question.'

The refusal spilled out without thought or effort and the realization staggered him.

Each day since his arrival he had vowed that the sooner he could leave the house in Abercromby Square the better he would be pleased, yet when Arabella was giving him the excuse he needed, he jumped like a scalded cat.

Was it for Sarah's sake he wanted so much to stay?

Surely not, he reasoned. It would have been the wisest thing he had ever done could he have removed himself from the despair of loving her.

'I cannot leave,' he repeated more calmly yet wondering still at his own perversity. 'My Aunt Norris is ill and I am very concerned about Adam, too.'

But it wasn't just Sarah or Adam or Aunt Hetty who kept him, thought Patrick. Something else held him; some secret truth hidden deep in his heart that defied recognition.

'Your aunt and your friend? Are they more important to you than me – than *us*?'

'Oh, my dear,' Patrick pleaded, 'you make it so difficult for me to explain.'

He took the dainty handkerchief she held and carefully patted her eyes.

'Look now; dry your tears and give me your hand. I will show you something. It will perhaps help you to understand.'

Reluctantly Arabella did as he asked.

'This,' said Patrick flatly as he opened the door of the small room nearest the surgery, 'is the dispensary.'

The brown laudanum bottle stood where he had left it little over an hour ago. The sun washed over it so that it glinted mockingly, reminding him of how he had hurt Sarah and in hurting her had driven a knife into his own heart.

'The dispensary?' Arabella repeated, glancing at its emptiness, sensing at once its inadequacy.

Patrick nodded, unspeaking, and urged her across the echoing hall and into the large room that ran from the front of the house to the back.

'This is the sick-ward,' he said, suddenly fiercely proud. 'Here, if there is an empty bed, no one is turned away. It is clean and sweet and a person may feel no sense of shame or indignity at being nursed here.'

He paused, startled by the depths of his feelings, willing Arabella to understand.

'The sick come to us not to die but to be made well. Often they are starving and penniless and their cares become our cares. There is little money here – Adam and Sarah depend upon the charity of many people – and there are few instruments or surgical aids to help them,' he said, recalling with a surge of happiness the triumph he and Sarah had shared when the Haggarty baby grasped at life with his tiny hands.

'Here at *The Haven*, a man is a doctor against all odds, Arabella. Here, Fate challenges a man to be a *real* doctor!'

Then suddenly and humbly Patrick realized the truth of his own dilemma. It came to him like a wild new awakening and it came in a blinding flash of truth.

No! he exulted, it wasn't just Sarah and Adam and Aunt Hetty who kept him at *The Haven*. Life had thrown him a challenge and he had picked it up because all his life he had been picking up challenges! He had unconsciously accepted the overwhelming odds against winning and he had so far survived because he had proved himself to be a good doctor. More than that, he had learned compassion. He had become a *real* doctor!

'Do you understand, Arabella?' he whispered joyfully, his eyes glowing with a happiness he could not explain but felt with delirious intensity.

'Could I leave *The Haven*? Could I leave these people?'

Arabella did not reply. Instead, she fought desperately to bite back the retort that sprung to her lips –

'What about my father and the duty you owe to him? What about me, Patrick, the woman you are to marry? Do you expect me to share this existence with you?'

She was about to fling those questions in his face but her instincts screamed out against it. She was treading on strange ground. Here was a different man, a man she had never known to exist. This was not the ambitious doctor eager to get on in the world and gather round him the riches that would loudly proclaim his success. This was not the polite genteel young doctor whose bedside manner was the delight of the rich old ladies.

Suddenly, it seemed, this strange new Patrick gloried in working himself to a standstill for little or no reward. He had become a crusader and seemed to find joy in it.

Take care, warned the woman in Arabella, *for this new creature will not be swayed by cajoling or tears!*

This man she must learn to know anew and suddenly she was aware that if she was to keep him she must fight for him and fight with every fibre of her being.

She turned her back on the sick-ward and walked towards the open front door.

'My trunks are outside, Patrick. Will you be so kind as to have them brought in for me?'

She gave him a sweet smile, womanly submissive, all traces of anger seemingly gone. 'If you will not come with me, dearest, then I must stay here, with you!'

The sudden about-face caught Patrick off balance. To realize in one wondrous moment that at last he knew his true purpose in life had left him in a state of tipsy elation.

But Arabella was about to thrust herself into that life and it was a sobering thought.

To stay at *The Haven* was all he wanted, now. To share the lot of Sarah and Adam, however much pain and heartache it might cause him to see them together, was one thing. To include Arabella in that life would be vastly difficult. But he realized that for the moment he was being offered a reprieve and much as it might complicate matters, he had no other alternative than to accept it.

'Very well, Arabella. I will let your papa know you are safe with me but I warn you that life at *The Haven* is not easy. There are no servants here, as such. We all serve, but only the sick. If you will accept those conditions you may stay here until other arrangements can be made, but you must expect no favours, Arabella. Life is rough, here – you can take it, or leave it . . .'

There was a small silence between them, then Arabella spoke.

'Thank you, Patrick. I will do my best not to hinder your work.'

Her reply was deceptively meek but inside her the turmoil of uncertainty raged with frightening intensity. Things would not go easily for her if she stayed at *The Haven*, she knew it only too well, for a glance at the Spartan bareness of the place confirmed that Patrick had spoken nothing but the truth and what was more, he meant every word of what he had said.

Life is rough, here . . . She accepted that and in doing so, realized with absolute certainty that if she did not accept such conditions and try for a little while to fit into the life of *The Haven*, she could lose Patrick forever. She must tread carefully and bide her time until she could make him see sense. When she had first arrived at the house she was sure that she had a woman for a rival but now it seemed to Arabella that Sarah Rigby could have been more easily disposed of than the intangible crusade that Patrick seemed determined to fight. No one, thought Arabella despairingly, could fight a *cause*!

So she smiled sweetly up at Patrick.

'Very well,' she affirmed, 'I am ready, dearest. Will you please have someone show me to my rooms?'

'But, Sarah,' Patrick protested as they sat together in the brief peace of the empty surgery, 'it is not right you should give up your bed yet again. You must take mine.'

'Thank you, Patrick, but no. You need your sleep and besides,' Sarah smiled impishly, 'the bed in your attic is the most uncomfortable in the whole house. I shall be quite happy sleeping in the kitchen. It will not be the first time I have slept on a mattress beneath the kitchen table. Miss Harrington is welcome to my bed.'

'It is so unfair,' Patrick persisted. 'Why must it always be you, Sarah, who is put out?'

Sarah gave a little shrug of her shoulders.

'Because I choose it to be so and anyway, I will be near the ward and nearer to Adam.'

Patrick smiled.

'You are right as you always are, Sarah Rigby. And you remind me that I have not made my round of the ward or visited my aunt, or Adam.'

'Your aunt seems much better and Adam was sleeping when last I looked into his room.'

She puckered her forehead into a worried frown.

'But I carried away his tray. He had not attempted to eat his food.'

'I am a great believer in the medicine of sleep, Sarah,' Patrick comforted. 'Don't worry. I will take a look at Adam as soon as he awakens.'

He rose to his feet, impatient to end their talk, be away from her disturbing presence, but Sarah remained seated.

'Is there something else?'

'Yes, Patrick, there is.'

Sarah dropped her eyes to the fingers that twisted anxiously on her lap.

'This afternoon – when I was crying and Miss Harrington arrived – I fear I caused you both embarrassment. I am very sorry about it and I am sorry I cried.'

She did not look at him as she spoke and Patrick was grateful for it. He did not want to see her troubled grey eyes, for to do so might release the words of love that were locked in his heart.

Instead he said, brusquely, 'That is all right, ma'am. Please do not mention it further.'

Sarah flinched inwardly, regretting almost that she had tried to thank him for his kindness. But Patrick was right to speak to her thus, she reasoned. Doubtless he was thinking that to offer more sympathy might encourage a fresh outburst of tears.

She shook her head impatiently. She would not cry again. No matter what happened, she could not and must not indulge in the luxury of tears. There was no time for weeping at *The Haven*.

She tilted her chin and said as brightly as she could, 'Miss Harrington is going to be a great blessing, Patrick. She is fetching and carrying and helping Molly in every possible way. I am truly grateful to her although it seems very wrong to allow a guest to work.'

Oh Sarah, Patrick's mind supplied, *you do not know Arabella as I know her. Today, this domesticity is just a game. By tomorrow it will have ceased to be a novelty and the friction between she and I will start again.*

'Arabella is hardly a guest, Sarah,' he returned tersely. 'She expressed a wish to stay and help us.'

'Then I am doubly grateful,' Sarah insisted.

Please, she pleaded inside her. *Please stay with us, Arabella. Don't go back to London for a little while. Don't take Patrick away from us – we need him so.*

She must try, she resolved, to make Miss Harrington's stay as bearable as she possibly could. She must show her gratitude to Arabella and try to see she did not work too hard and tire herself, for without Patrick's help Sarah thought despairingly, she could not carry on.

Arabella let her weary body sag onto the low, hard bed and fumbled to unfasten the too-large apron that covered her dress.

From the bed opposite she could feel Kate Tarleton's eyes upon her and wished there was a screen behind which she might undress in privacy.

Bending forward to unhook the row of buttons on her boots she felt her ringlets damp and limp against her face. Her feet throbbed and it would be good, she thought, to wiggle her toes and rest her aching leggs.

Arabella realized with a little smile of triumph that distressing as the work had been, at least it had caused the occupants of *The Haven* to take notice of her.

'Sure, it's not right for a dainty wee creature like

yourself to be doing the work of a serving girl!' Molly had protested.

And Patrick had smiled grimly as she hurried past him with gruel for the old lady in the corner bed in the sick-ward. Was he regretting his insistence that she should make herself useful? Had it startled him to realize that she could not be frightened away by the threat of a little housework? Patrick would give in, vowed Arabella, before *she* would!

A dainty white boot fell to the floor with a thump and Arabella recalled the undisguised admiration in the eyes of the funny little one-legged man as he called her a pretty little flower.

Sarah Rigby, too, had expressed her gratitude, imploring her not to tire herself and to take a rest and a dish of tea. Sarah Rigby, thought Arabella, had been the cause of serious concern to her. To see her in Patrick's arms had sent pangs of jealous anger stabbing through her.

But she need not have worried, she realized, for Sarah Rigby was plain and ordinary with her screwed-up hair and sad, grey eyes. It was almost feasible to believe now that Patrick really had been comforting her. Arabella was surprised that to recall the scene no longer made her angry; only regretful that she had been foolish enough to lose her temper and scream at Patrick like a fishwife.

Sarah Rigby was no threat; she did not, Arabella decided, have to fear the careworn, quiet woman she had found in Patrick's arms. She knew where the danger lay and she was at a loss as yet to know how to deal with it. Her real enemy, Arabella knew, was *The Haven*; the great bare house where the sick found health again or died with dignity amidst love and care. She knew that if she were not to lose Patrick she must fight not a woman but a way of life that she could not yet even begin to understand.

Perplexed and anxious she turned to face Kate Tarleton, forcing a small smile as she met the undisguised look of wonder.

The wide brown eyes dropped to gaze at the bedcover.

'Begging your pardon, miss; I know it's rude to stare but you've got me fair mystified.'

'Oh?'

'Aye, miss. Why's the likes of you doing servant's work and why aren't you creating at having to sleep in the same room with the likes of me?'

'Why shouldn't I help with the work here?' Arabella was immediately on the defensive.

Why, why, *why* must everybody presume that she was useless? They were all like her papa who teased and petted her as if she were still a child.

'And why shouldn't I share a room with you?' she flung at the startled girl.

Kate's pinched little face flushed. She dropped her eyes again and for a time there was an uncomfortable silence in the small, hot attic.

Then Arabella spoke.

'I'm sorry. I didn't mean to snap. Are you feeling better now after your accident?'

For reasons she could not explain, Arabella wanted to know more about the girl whose room she shared.

'Yes, miss, I thank you, but I'd have been dead in a pool of me own blood, now,' she supplied dramatically, 'if it hadn't been for Doctor Norris.'

Arabella blushed with pleasure.

'Doctor Norris and I are soon to be married,' she said proudly.

Kate Tarleton's eyes took on a wistful expression.

'Don't suppose anybody'll ever want to wed me.'

'Why not?'

'Well, on account of me being what I am — what I *was*,' she corrected hastily.

She looked pleadingly into Arabella's eyes.

'Did they tell you I was on the streets, miss? That's how I got knifed and battered last night. But Miss Sarah says I've finished with all that. Says as how she'll chain me to the table-leg afore she'll let me go on the game again. Miss Sarah's going to find me a position with a good family when I'm mended and then I'll be respectable.'

Her eyes shone.

'Just imagine that — being in gentleman's service; eating regular and sleeping in a bed . . .'

'Was it awful, doing what you did?' Arabella asked.

It was strange, she thought, but Kate didn't look like a street-woman — at least not what Cissy, her father's kitchen-maid said street-women looked like. Arabella had learned a great many of the unlady-like facts of life in whispered conversations in the Harley Street kitchens and Kate did not fit in with any of Cissy's lurid descriptions of wantonness.

Kate nodded.

'Aye, it's an awful life but at least I ain't got rot-gut. I'm thankful for that!'

Arabella tried hard to be shocked by such frankness but could not. She found instead a deep sympathy within her for Kate's misfortunes. It was a feeling that was new to Arabella Harrington and she was not at all sure she fully understood it.

'How old are you, Kate?'

'Thirteen or fourteen, I think. I've no way of knowing exactly, me Ma and Da being dead.'

Arabella swallowed hard. Kate was alone in the world; it must be a terrible thing, she thought.

She wondered how often in the past she herself, despite the luxury with which she was surrounded, had felt lonely, too. How often, she mused, if she had been given a wish, would she have asked for a sister or brother, perhaps?

Kate Tarleton had no one and no home; she had no money either, unless she got it *that* way.

Arabella was well aware of the fact that no young lady should begin to understand the plight of one so unfortunate. She should not even speak to such a person, let alone feel pity for her.

Yet she felt pity for Kate Tarleton; pity for her poor bruised face and the life she had been forced to lead, but mostly she felt sad at Kate's loneliness. Arabella could understand loneliness but she knew that if she lay awake the whole of the night she could not even begin to imagine the degradation of the life the young girl had been forced to lead.

Sarah Rigby and Patrick had brought Kate to *The Haven*. They had taken her from the Liverpool gutters and were caring for her with compassion. What had Patrick said?

' . . . *their cares become our cares*.'

And they would not allow Kate to go back to the uncaring streets. They would find her a position in a gentleman's household and the thought of it made Kate's eager young eyes shine with pride.

How dreadful must her life have been when the prospect of a life of domestic service seemed like the promise of Utopia? How could anybody like being a servant? she wondered. She had fetched and carried for just half a day and her body ached with fatigue. And tomorrow would be exactly the same. Tomorrow would be . . .

She shut down her thoughts and surrendered her body to the cool caress of clean cotton sheets. Her aching back did not feel the lumpiness of the mattress. Instead, she felt a strange thrill of achievement singing through her body.

Tomorrow would be a new day, she thought wonderingly; a chance to start again and make atonement; a day not to be allowed to slip by uselessly. Tomorrow she could, in some small measure, show gratitude for those things she had in such abundance. She could try to help those who were less fortunate than herself and less able to help themselves.

It wasn't really a question of showing them that Arabella Harrington could rise to a challenge and prove herself.

She wasn't quite sure just what she wanted of tomorrow so bewildering were the thoughts that spun with giddy joy in her head. She was certain only of one thing: that she felt pity and compassion and love within her for the first time and she wanted, most humbly, to be allowed to share them.

She hoped wistfully that she could give Patrick cause to be proud of her.

She leaned over and blew out the candle.

'Good night, Kate,' she whispered. 'God bless you . . .'

Nine

Through the thin partition wall, not a foot away from the sleeping Arabella, Patrick lay on his bed and looked up at the skylight above him into the dark of the night.

What a mess it all was, he thought. At last he knew that the only thing he wanted in life was to work at *The Haven* yet the realisation had come too late, he fretted.

His longing to care for the people of the alleys and back-streets was beyond all doubt but he had a duty to Doctor Harrington and to Arabella whom he had asked to become his wife.

Patrick knew now that he could willingly forsake the opulent life of Harley Street but how easy would it be for him to be free of it?

Doctor Harrington might well insist that he return and honour his agreement – he would be well within his rights – and Arabella was betrothed to him. A gentleman did not break his word, did he?

But Arabella could never fit into the life at *The Haven* no matter how she tried, his tortured mind supplied. True, he admitted as he thumped his hot pillow yet again, Arabella had surprised him by her willingness to help. He had never before known her to perform one menial task but then, she had never before had the need to.

What could be behind Arabella's actions? What, he reasoned, could she be trying to prove?

Patrick levered himself into a sitting position. Tonight, sleep evaded him. His body was weary but his mind buzzed with irritations and problems. Would it not be better, he thought, if he were to try to find one or two newly-qualified physicians who had not the means to buy their own practices yet would welcome the chance to gain experience at *The Haven*? He could return to London, then. He could afford to make an allowance to Aunt Hetty so that she never need work again and he would marry Arabella as he was pledged to do. He could try to forget Sarah; forget that she and Adam were in love. If he were away from it all he would not be tormented by Sarah's troubled grey eyes or feel the urge to lay her work-roughened hands to his cheek. If he could accept that there was no place in Sarah's life for him it would make it all the easier to leave.

But if there were no young physicians to be obtained, if Adam did not get well again, what then would happen to the poor ones? They would still need him, Patrick knew, just as desperately as he needed *them*. He was one of them; they were his own people. He had been reared among them in the tight, airless streets. It seemed that no matter who his real parents were the courts and alleys of Liverpool had set their mark on him and now they were calling him back. How could he have been so blind as to ever think he could forsake them?

With an exclamation of annoyance Patrick fumbled to light the candle at his bedside. The fingers of his pocket-watch pointed to three o'clock and soon it would be dawn and the start of another hot, dreary day. Soon the streets would be astir with people and the pathetic huddle of men and women would gather at *The Haven* once more.

He wondered how the cholera-ridden warehouses and

cellars had fared during the long-drawn night and how many more souls had departed their miserable bodies for want of care that might have saved them. Now the infirmaries were packed tight and Doctor Duncan had commandeered two ships and had them anchored out in the wide river to take the poor wretches who had nowhere to die and to prevent, if only in small measure, the further spread of the evil.

Patrick reached for his coat and slipped it over his nightshirt. He had not been happy when he visited Adam at bedtime. He had had the feeling that his friend had been holding back, deliberately trying to mislead him. Adam refused to let Patrick take his temperature saying that he had taken it himself and found it quite satisfactory.

But Patrick knew Adam had not eaten all day and when he suggested that Adam might like to meet Arabella there had been a too-hasty refusal.

'A sick-room is no please for pleasantries, Patrick. Leave it for a little while, will you? Perhaps tomorrow?'

But for all that, Adam had wanted to talk about other things. He had talked about *The Haven* and of his fears that one day there might be no one to care for the sick, save Sarah herself.

Patrick had challenged the statement.

'Why do you say that, Adam? Am I not able to run *The Haven* for a little longer? With rest you will get well again. If you would only give yourself a chance . . .'

'Patrick, we are not talking about my miserable consumptive lungs, now.'

'Then what?'

A dart of fear shivered through Patrick.

'Sometimes I think time is so short for me,' Adam shook his head wearily. 'It is then that I know only a desperate feeling of failure. I worry too, about Sarah. I know so little about her, Patrick. Until now it had not mattered to me who she was or where she came from, but if I were to die . . .'

'Stop it, Adam. Stop it, I say!'

' . . . *if I were to die*,' Adam insisted quietly, 'what would become of Sarah? I think above all I care about leaving her.'

'Then if you are determined to harbour such morbid thoughts, Adam, let me say at once that in my opinion Sarah would be able to care for herself.'

'But, Patrick,' Adam protested weakly, 'I am the tenant of this house. I live here only because some saintly person does not demand the months of rent I owe him. It would not bode well for Sarah and Molly and Dicky-Sam if I were not here. They might be tumbled into the street without a second thought. What would happen to Sarah, then?'

Patrick reached for Adam's hand. It was like the vulnerable hand of a small, trusting child and it shocked him it could be so cold whilst at the same time beads of sweat glistened on Adam's forehead.

'Listen to me, friend. You are tired and unwell. It is natural that you should feel despondent at times, but if it will comfort you I give you my most solemn word that you need never fear for the welfare of Sarah or Molly or Dicky-Sam. That at least I can promise you.'

Adam nodded his head and more relieved, smiled his sweet smile, a smile that tore at Patrick's heart. In Adam's beloved face was reflected all the sadness and gladness of their youth together. In it, Patrick was reminded of their burning optimism and of his own betrayal of those long-ago hopes. His voice unsteady with emotion he said, 'What are you keeping back from me, Adam? Why will you not let me examine you? Are you hiding something? I am your old friend and I know you almost as well as I know myself. Tell me what is really causing this brooding?'

But Adam closed his eyes against Patrick's directness.

'Leave me be, Patrick. Let me sleep?'

For the moment Patrick knew there was nothing more to be said but fear had coursed through him with ice-cold intensity.

He measured a strong sleeping-draught and was relieved that Adam took it without protest, whispering quietly, 'I shall sleep, now. Goodnight, Patrick, my dear friend. God keep you.'

So reluctantly and apprehensively Patrick had left Adam's bedside, fear nagging inside him that he could not explain.

Now suddenly in the small, cold hours of the morning, a feeling of animal terror gripped Patrick and he knew why sleep was evading him. Adam, he was certain, was in need of help. He would go downstairs to the sick-room and he would know at once if the morbid fears had any substance. Shielding the candle-flame with his hand he gently pushed open the bedroom door, sensing at once that Adam was not asleep.

'Patrick? Thank God you have come!'

'Adam – what is it?'

Fear surged afresh through Patrick, then wound itself into a tight ball in his throat so that he could hardly speak. He bent to light the bedside candle from his own and as it flickered then flamed into light he knew his most awful fears were realized.

Jerking in spasms of agony Adam lay flushed and sweating. His breath came in small painful gasps and Patrick wanted to puke with fear as a dreaded and familiar stench filled his nostrils.

Desperately he tried to raise the pathetic body into a comfortable position but Adam grasped his hands.

'Remember your promise, Patrick.'

Each word seemed an agony of effort.

'Take care of Sarah for me . . .'

The frail shoulders shook with a spasm of coughing.

' . . . take care of them all –'

Patrick wiped the fevered brow, bending low so that his lips were close to Adam's ear.

'Don't be afraid, Adam. I will awaken Sarah. I'll bring her to you.'

He did not remember his flight through the quietly brooding house or of groping with his hands for Sarah's shoulders in the unaccustomed darkness of the kitchen. He knew only that Adam was ill, desperately so and that Sarah must be with him.

'Wake up, Sarah. Wake up!'

Dimly Patrick saw her shake her head as if trying to remember where she lay but she did not cry out in alarm. Years of sudden night calls had schooled a discipline into her and her actions were almost automatic as she reached for the wrap that lay beside her.

Patrick turned his back on her and thrust a splinter of wood into the near-dead fire, blowing on it until it burst into sudden flame. Then, lighting the hanging oil lamp he turned again to Sarah.

She stood, endearingly vulnerable, her shawl clutched about her, blinking her eyes awake. She gave a little smile of recognition.

'Oh, it's you, Patrick. Is anything the matter?'

He placed his hands on her shoulders, urging his strength into her.

'Sarah?'

With an effort she raised her head.

'I am sorry, Patrick, but I am so tired . . .'

Compassion flowed through him as he realized that what he was about to tell her would send her small precious world crashing into smithereens at her feet.

'Sarah, I want you to come with me to Adam.'

He felt the sudden tremor of fear that ran through her body.

'What is it?'

Instantly she was awake, stumbling on bare feet across the stone-flagged floor.

'Is Adam worse?' she breathed.

For a moment Patrick was taken aback by her sudden wakefulness then instinctively he threw his body between her and the doorway.

'Listen, my dear. You must compose yourself before you go to Adam – you must be brave . . .'

Sarah's voice rose to a frightened sob as she struggled to get past him.

'Adam, oh, Adam! What is it? Tell me, Patrick?'

Gently Patrick restrained her frantic struggles, wanting with all his heart not to have to tell her. He sought her eyes then held them with the agonized intensity of his gaze.

'Sarah,' he whispered softly. 'Adam is worse; he's got cholera. I think he is dying.'

Dying? Adam dying?

For a moment in time that was no more than the blinking of an eyelid yet which stretched into a lifetime of horror, Sarah's world stood petrified.

'No! Oh, please, *please*, no!'

She was standing outside her body now and the agonized whisper she heard had surely not been hers?

But strangely her lips moved; stiff cold lips in a stiff, cold face. She looked into Patrick's eyes and read

compassion there; read too that her plea was little more
than a vain hope.

'I must go to him! Please let me go to him?' that
strange voice whispered.

Now the lamp that hung from the ceiling had joined
in the nightmare, casting shadowy, menacing fingers to a
floor that rocked beneath her feet.

Desperately she clung for support to Patrick's hands
willing her mind to control her shaking body, closing
her eyes against the room that slid and spun around her.

She drew in a shuddering breath, fighting the darkness
that threatened to engulf her and to which she so desperately wanted to surrender.

'Hold me? Hold me, Patrick?'

Once more Sarah felt the comfort and strength of
Patrick's arms about her. With blessed relief she laid her
head on his chest and heard his voice calling her back to
sanity.

'It is all right, Sarah. You are not alone. I am here; I
will help you.'

Oh, my dearest, his heart yearned, *I want always to
help you. I want to care for you and comfort you and
never let the world hurt you again. I would exchange
destinies with Adam this instant if it could give you back
your happiness.*

'I'll send Molly to you,' he said, instead. 'You are cold
with shock and she will help you to dress.'

He held her at arm's length, looking into her eyes,
willing his strength and love into her frightened heart.
Perhaps, Patrick thought, the simple action of dressing,
of pulling on her boots and pinning up her hair would
give her the time she needed to compose herself a little,
come to terms with the cruel truth he had just hurled at
her.

'I must go back to Adam,' Patrick said softly, cupping Sarah's face in hands gentle with compassion. 'When you are ready, come to him. It is you he wants now. He needs your comfort and love. Try to be brave, for his sake?'

A small smile flicked on Sarah's lips and once again Patrick saw that familiar, endearing tilting of her chin.

'Thank you,' she whispered, drawing in a deep breath. 'I will be all right, now.'

Molly set down the teapot with a clatter, grateful that a new day was breaking, wishing at the same time that it were still yesterday and the events of the night had not happened.

She hesitated for a moment, reluctant to ask the question.

'It's cholera that Doctor Adam's got, then?' she whispered.

'Yes, Molly.'

'And he's bad?'

'Yes,' Patrick confirmed bitterly, 'he's very ill.'

'I tried to stop him!' Tears misted Molly's eyes and her lower lip trembled. 'I wanted him to stay in his bed when the sick from the *Cornucopia* came but nothing would do but that he should get up and attend to them.'

She sniffed and wiped the tears from her cheeks in an appealing, childlike gesture.

'Miss Sarah is afeard of that ship, Doctor Patrick.'

'I'm beginning to dislike it myself, Molly.'

Now, the *Cornucopia* had been turned into a hospital for the cholera sick, for infirmaries were turning away patients to die in the streets, so overcrowded were their wards. So Doctor Duncan had had the ship comman-

deered and towed out into mid-river where she now
floated at anchor to take on yet more miserable victims of
the dreaded fever.

Perhaps, Patrick thought, when the nightmare was over
and the port returned to some semblance of normality,
some sane person would have the sense to order the ship
to be fired and exorcize for all time the evil that seemed to
have seeped into her very timbers.

'You'll tell Dicky-Sam not to eat his food without
scrubbing his hands, won't you Molly?' Patrick asked,
'and I'll make you a solution of calcium-chloride to act as
a disinfectant.'

'A *disinfectant*, sir?'

'It will kill any cholera germs that might get onto your
hands.'

It was hard for Patrick to explain to people like Molly
O'Keefe such strange words as disinfect, or germ. Even
the medical profession was only just beginning to
acknowledge their existence and importance.

'I see, doctor,' Molly acknowledged doubtfully.

At least, thought Patrick grimly, simple though her
heart was she had the right idea, for cleanliness was
almost a religion with Molly.

'And you know that the house must be thoroughly
cleansed? The hall, the surgery – wherever the
Cornucopia sick have been – even the benches they sat on
– all must be scrubbed, then scrubbed again.'

'Aye, doctor; Miss Sarah told me. She's away now,
seeing to the sulphur candles you want lit.'

Molly sighed.

'You know, we're lucky at *The Haven*. At least there's
always water in our taps. That's more'n some folk have
got! At least we can keep ourselves clean here.'

She was right, thought Patrick. There just wasn't

enough water for everyone in the town. Even if people could be educated to understand the importance of cleanliness, it would do little good. How could people be clean in those miserable hovels and rat-ridden cellars when a communal stand-tap dripped water for one reluctant hour out of every day?

'Is Miss Harrington awake yet, Molly?'

'That she is, doctor, and up and dressed this last half-hour.'

It was only then that Patrick realized with apprehension the danger to which Arabella was now exposed. He wondered if he should demand that she leave for London immediately where she would be safe from the risk of infection.

He wished with all his heart she had not come to *The Haven*. There were difficulties enough without having the wellbeing of his employer's only child to add to his worries.

Patrick gazed upwards to the pavement outside the kitchen window, watching disembodied feet and the wheels of a milk-seller's cart as they trundled past.

Here was dawning another day. Not so long ago Patrick would have viewed it with trepidation. Now there was nothing he wanted more than to spend each day working at *The Haven* with Adam and Sarah.

But it could never be, for Adam was ill – dangerously so – and he, Patrick, had long ago chosen another path; one which eventually he would have to tread again.

Slowly he rose to his feet, reluctant to leave the saneness of Molly's kitchen but knowing it was time to visit Adam again.

Sarah would be sitting by his bed in that bare little room and the sight of her grief-stricken face would tumble his heart afresh. And Patrick knew he would have to listen to Adam's delirious mutterings and watch and wait helplessly until the crisis was reached.

Meantime, there would be another surgery to take, the sick in the ward to be visited and medicines to be dispensed. There was so much to be done at *The Haven* – too much – but then, thought Patrick grimly, there always had been and it had been done without complaint.

Now, Adam had driven himself to death's doorstep and with no thought for herself, Sarah was nursing him. The realization of Sarah's danger sent a shiver of fear surging through Patrick and he quickened his steps that he might be near her again.

A familiar acrid smell choked in his nostrils, causing him to cough violently and he realized that Sarah had already lighted the sulphur candles. Through the open door of the ward he could hear the steady rhythm of a scrubbing-brush against bare wood.

'Arabella!' he gasped.

She was kneeling beside a pail of steaming water, a bar of soap in one hand, an unwieldy brush in the other and determinedly scrubbing the floor of the ward. She rose to her feet as Patrick entered, her hair tied back in an unbecoming knot, her hands red and swollen from the unaccustomed immersion in hot suds.

'What on earth are you doing?' he asked, incredulously.

Placing her finger to her lips Arabella beckoned Patrick to follow her.

Closing the door of the ward behind her she wiped her hands on her apron before asking quietly,

'Doctor Carmichael has contracted cholera – am I right?'

Patrick nodded.

'Yes, Arabella, you are right and I am forced to the conclusion that *The Haven* is no safe place for you. I think it would be better if you were to return to London at once.'

'I see.'

Arabella set her lips in the way that was so familiar to Patrick yet now there was a sadness in her eyes, too.

'Are you in a position to send me back to London?'

'What do you mean?'

'Look, Patrick, there is cholera in the house. Miss Rigby is nursing Doctor Carmichael so cannot be of any help to you. There are sick to be cared for, a surgery to run and now the house must be thoroughly cleansed against the spread of the infection.'

She paused, seeking his eyes with her own, willing him to accept the soundness of her reasoning.

'Am I not right?' she demanded, quietly.

'Yes, Arabella, but I cannot let you stay here. I am responsible for your welfare – I have a duty to your father.'

'And I too have a duty, Patrick, to the man I am to marry. It entitles me to to stay by his side and share his cares. I will *not* go back to London!'

Patrick opened his mouth to protest then closed it again, unspeaking. Could this be Arabella Harrington who spoke such good sense so quietly? Was the woman who scrubbed floors that same person he had asked to become his wife? He had to admit to himself that all she said was right but he had expected a tantrum when he had suggested she should leave *The Haven* and there hadn't been one. She had completely mystified him.

'Very well, Arabella, you are right, I suppose.'

He gave a small shrug of resignation then chided himself immediately for his ingratitude.

'I will be glad of your help,' he hastened.

'Oh, Patrick, I will do anything . . .' she whispered eagerly, a new humility in her voice.

She raised her eyes to his, silently asking him to pull down the invisible barrier that seemed always to be between them now.

' . . . only tell me how I can be of help.'

Ashamed of his churlish behaviour, Patrick bent down and gently kissed her cheek.

'Thank you, my dear,' was all he could bring himself to say.

Lord, what a mess it all is, he thought as he watched Arabella walk back to the ward, the dejected droop of her shoulders telling him that she too was as unhappy and bewildered as he was.

'Where will it all end?' Patrick whispered to the emptiness of the hall. 'What in heaven's name has gone wrong with the world?'

Like a small child in need of comfort he made for Hetty Norris's room for there, he hoped, he could snatch a few moments in which to gather together his thoughts. Aunt Hetty always understood.

She was sitting up in bed like a chirpy little sparrow when Patrick entered her room.

'There you are at long last, boy! I thought you'd never come! I want to get up. It's time for me to go back home.'

'That is out of the question, Aunt Hetty. There have already been three deaths in Lace Street from cholera. To go back would be madness.'

'Is it so very bad, then?'

'Yes, Aunt – we have an epidemic on our hands and the heat is making things worse.'

It was obvious to Patrick that Hetty Norris had not yet

been told of Adam's illness. He said, 'Adam is very sick, Aunt Hetty.'

A look of fear fleeted across the old face.

'Cholera?' she asked, tersely.

Reluctantly Patrick nodded.

'I am going to visit him now. I came to see you first – to explain that it will be better if I don't visit you too often until the danger is over. Arabella will look after you and explain what is best to be done to stop the spreading of the infection.'

'I understand, boy. I understand,' Hetty Norris whispered quietly. 'Is there anything at all a useless old body like me can do to help?'

'No, Aunt, there is little any of us can do now but wait. But you can pray for Adam. Pray for him, I beg of you, with all your heart.'

But no prayers could help Adam Carmichael.

Quietly and gently as he had lived, so he slipped away from life as the first star of evening shimmered in a darkening sky.

Gently Patrick released the fingers entwined in Sarah's and closed the sightless eyes.

'Sarah?' he whispered fearfully for she sat as still and cold as marble, her face set in a mask of disbelief.

'So quick,' she whispered. 'It was so quick. He didn't have a chance . . .'

'It is often that way, Sarah,' Patrick replied, his voice thick with anguish and despair. 'It is the only blessing that cholera brings with it. Adam was already a sick man; he had little within him with which to fight.'

He waited for the torrent of grief to burst from Sarah's

lips but it did not come. Instead, she rose slowly to her feet and almost reverently drew the bed-sheet over Adam's face. Her actions were automatic as if some unseen manipulator pulled strings that gave movement to her wooden limbs.

Gently Patrick placed his arm around her shoulders drawing her from Adam's bedside and from the room wanting her to weep so that he might weep with her but she walked away from him, her head held bravely high, preparing herself to do those tasks that must be done with quiet dignity.

Perhaps she would cry later, Patrick thought. He hoped she would for it was not good to harbour grief. But Sarah's unhappiness was a private thing, he knew. In her own time and in her own way she would surrender to it and pity surged through him afresh for the quiet woman he had come to love.

Ten

It was long past midnight and Patrick's body ached with mingled shock and fatigue for the work of healing must take precedence over death.

Now, in a house hushed with grief, they talked sadly of Adam.

'There must be no public mourning,' Sarah said as she sat with Patrick in the surgery that had once been Adam's.

'He would not want fuss – he told me that. He said it with such certainty that now I think he must have known . . .'

Her voice trailed away into a desolate whisper and for a moment she did not speak but sat staring ahead, seeing nothing but a blank, black wall of misery.

'Adam was sometimes saddened by all the pomp and ceremony of a funeral,' she continued. 'He felt it was wrong to spend so much money in death when it could have done so much more good in life. "When I die," he once said, "give me a pauper's coffin and lay me with the poor ones, Sarah."'

She spoke softly, a slight tremor in her voice but her eyes were still empty of the tears that might have brought some small comfort.

Patrick nodded silently. He understood what Sarah was trying to say.

To be laid to rest with pomp and ceremony was the

burning desire of rich and poor alike. Those who had the means made a great pageantry of the giving back of their dead. Even the poor insisted upon their sad moments of glory, making beggars of themselves to the men who ran the infamous burial clubs.

Adam had been saddened at the waste of it all and now, Patrick vowed, Adam should have his wish.

'I know what he was trying to tell you, Sarah, and I agree with you. We will respect his wishes, you and I. We will lay him beside his poor ones as he would have wanted. There is no shame in a pauper's coffin – all men are equal in death. Adam tried to show that men are equal in life, too, but few cared to listen to him.'

Patrick shook his head wearily.

'I was one of those men,' he whispered, bitterly.

But even in the fever-ridden port where the sultry heat made the burial of the cholera dead an almost indecent necessity of haste, Adam's poor ones remembered. When the first shock of disbelief had given way to a despairing sorrow, their only thought was to honour their beloved Doctor Adam.

Not for him the indignity of a pit-burial, for dissolute and evil as the rum-sodden grave-diggers were, they showed their love for the gentle young doctor who had been their friend and set their spades grimly into the dry hard earth without thought of reward.

No city alderman or wealthy shipowner was borne to rest with more dignity than was Adam Carmichael as the people of the mean streets defied the order forbidding public gatherings and waited in silent misery outside the house in Abercromby Square.

And as Adam was laid on a simple carrier's cart that someone with love had bedecked with greenery, women wept and men set their lips in sorrow as he was borne away from the house from which no one in need had ever been sent away.

No fine carriages followed in the wake of the creaking little cart but men in rough working clothes and women, heads bowed in grief, walked sadly with their barefoot children to pay a last tribute of love.

No wailing mute carried his black-drapped staff but a one-legged little seaman with a grief-contorted face limped proudly at the head of the long, sad procession.

Head high, Sarah too walked with pride, fiercely glad for Adam's sake for the support of his loved ones.

Patrick stared ahead of him, his eyes not leaving the rough coffin and from all sides the soft sound of sobbing, of whispered prayers for the gentle young soul that was gone from them and small, unbelieving cries.

'What is to become of us, now?'

'Who can we turn to?'

'Who will care?'

I *care*, thought Patrick passionately. I want to try to take Adam's place. I want to do as he did and give as he gave but I am bonded to my master in London and held by a marriage-pledge I cannot but honour.

Adam was dead but the poor ones had a right to ask who would be left to care.

He wished that men were allowed to weep for his heart was bursting with unshed tears and his conscience was heavy as lead.

Adam was gone. He had forsaken the sweet Scottish island of his birth and made Liverpool his own and the brash, roistering port had taken him to its heart. He would rest, for ever a part of it now, in his pauper's coffin in the little cemetery by the Alms-houses, just two streets away from Abercromby Square.

'God keep you,' Patrick whispered as the earth received Adam Carmichael. 'Forgive me, dear friend, for breaking faith.'

Later that night as he sat alone in the darkening surgery and *The Haven* had settled down to a quietness born of sorrow, Patrick tried to take stock of the situation. His brain was so tired he could not think and his body ached, for the surgery had been more than ever crowded that night.

Many of those who came were not sick but had called to offer sympathy and to ask, timidly, what was to happen now that Doctor Adam was gone.

More than ever now Patrick knew how greatly Adam had been loved. Adam had been a champion, a shelter in a storm. Small wonder the house in Abercromby Square had come to be called *The Haven*.

Now Adam's poor ones were pleading for reassurance that his work would go on; that there should be someone else still to care.

Patrick set down his empty mug and walked slowly through the sighing house into the darkening garden. Outside, it was only a little less hot than in the oppressive atmosphere of *The Haven* but at least he could escape the choking fumes of the sulphur candles, the everlasting scrubbing of floors and boiling of bed-linen.

It was wrong of him to feel as he did when everyone was working until they were ready to sleep on their feet. It had been a bad day for them all but now Patrick knew he must come to terms with the future.

If only he could make Doctor Harrington understand how desperately important it was that the work at *The Haven* should go on, he thought.

But if by some miracle he should be allowed to have his wish, how would Arabella take to such a life? That he must honour his pledge and marry Arabella could not be denied but their marriage would be a sham because wherever he went or how far, Patrick knew that Sarah Rigby's sad-eyed wraith would always be at his side.

At first he tried to close his ears to the sound of Arabella's voice, needing as he did some time apart with his problems, wanting to be free from outside pressures and influences. He had come into the garden to be alone for a little while and stand where he and Sarah stood. Arabella's presence was an intrusion, he thought bitterly.

'Patrick?' she called again. 'Where are you?'

A sense of urgency in her voice made him call out, 'Here, by the statue!'

'Oh, please come. I don't know what to do but she's very sick, I'm sure of it. Sarah is ill now, Patrick!'

'Where is she?' he flung over his shoulder as he took the flight of stone steps in one desperate leap.

Sarah was standing in the hall, one hand grasping the newel-post at the foot of the staircase, the other stretched out to him in a gesture of supplication.

'Patrick?' she whispered, swaying on her feet as she tried to walk towards him. 'Help me, Patrick?'

Then her eyelids closed and she crumpled into a pathetic, unconscious huddle at his feet.

'Sarah!'

Anxiously Patrick rubbed her hands and patted her cheeks. Her flushed face, as he touched it, burned with a dry, intense heat.

'*Sarah?*' he pleaded as he gathered her into his arms, '*Oh, Sarah, my darling . . .*'

Her body was limp against him, her head rested beneath his chin.

Patrick stared unseeing into Arabella's eyes, knowing nothing and feeling nothing save that he had just plunged headlong into another nightmare.

How sick Sarah was he couldn't tell but his heart thumped against his ribs and his breath rasped harshly in his throat as he almost ran with her limp body to the sick-ward.

Gently he laid her on the one empty bed. Ahead of him the night stretched, long and desolate.

'I promise, Arabella, that as soon as I am able I will join you in London.'

Patrick looked despairingly at the litter of trunks and hat-boxes that were being carried to the waiting cab.

'You have said that before, Patrick,' Arabella replied sadly. 'How am I to believe that you mean what you say this time?'

Patrick winced, for the quiet finality of her reply hurt him far more than the most vicious of body-blows could ever have done. He looked into Arabella's eyes and saw that they were etched with tiny, tired lines. Her bobbing ringlets had been brushed straight and twisted into an unbecoming pleat in the nape of her neck. She looked older and suddenly strangely wiser as if she had faced life for the first time and was still reeling from the encounter.

Deliberately she avoided his eyes, pulling on her gloves with exaggerated care and Patrick saw that her hands were still red and swollen. He wanted to tell her how sorry he was that her stay at *The Haven* should have been so unhappy but there was a barrier of mistrust between them now and the words of explanation he tried to make came hard to his lips.

'Dearest, I give you my word that as soon as Miss Rigby is well enough to be left I will find another doctor to take charge here. I will come then and give an account of myself to your father. Believe me, Arabella, I will come.'

'And to me, Patrick? Will you give an account of your-self to *me*?' she whispered.

A flush of unease stained the back of Patrick's neck.

Not now? he pleaded, inwardly. He didn't want to provoke another scene. The night had been long and anxious and Sarah had tossed in a burning fever. He had not been able to diagnose her illness and he was in no mood for recriminations. And soon, he knew, Doctor Duncan might arrive. It wouldn't do for Doctor Duncan to witness Arabella in one of her moods nor, for that matter, see one of his old pupils in the throes of abandoned despair and that, he promised himself grimly, could take place at any moment.

But it was himself who shook with uncontrolled be-wilderment; Arabella was composed and dignified. It seemed, almost, as if she had left her childish ways behind her and that he was looking for the first time at Arabella, the woman.

He said, uncertainly, 'Please Arabella, bear with me for just a little longer. All will be well, I promise.'

'And you will not return with me to London?'

'I *cannot*! In two or three days, perhaps, but not now. Try to understand, I beg of you.'

'I have tried very hard to understand, Patrick. I have tried to help, to make you proud of me.'

Her voice trembled and for a moment she fought to control her emotions.

'I can do no more, my dear,' she said, eventually. 'I cannot stay here another day. It is up to you, now.'

She lifted her chin and forced a small smile to her lips.

'What ever you decide to do, I will try to understand, Patrick.'

Gently she kissed her fingertips then placed them to his lips.

'Don't keep me too long in uncertainty, I beg of you,' she said softly. Then she turned abruptly and walked quickly away as though reluctant to prolong the pain of their parting.

Patrick stood in the open doorway. He should, he knew, have handed her into the cab but he was unwilling to risk even the slightest rebuff. He waited instead for some small sign, some quick smile of understanding or a nod of goodbye.

But it did not come. The cab door slammed with a dreadful finality and Arabella did not even turn her head as she drove away.

Suddenly Patrick felt the need for comfort. His world had turned a somersault and landed in fragments at his feet. It seemed as he stood there that he was no longer capable of coherent thoughts.

Arabella had left and Sarah was ill. He had never, he thought, felt so bewildered or unsure in the whole of his life.

But Aunt Hetty would understand. To her he could pour out his tangled thoughts and she would listen as she always did as he arranged them into some semblance of order again. Aunt Hetty was wise beyond understanding he thought gratefully as he walked slowly up the stairs, unhappy and bewildered as a small, whipped child.

'What is it, boy?' Hetty Norris asked gently, instantly sensing his misery.

Mutely Patrick shook his head, lowering his body into

the bedside chair, closing his eyes to shut out the madness of his world.

For a little time the old woman did not speak, her heart sad at the sight of Patrick's pale, tormented face. Then she said,

'How is Sarah this morning?'

'She's sick aunt, very sick,' he whispered. 'Her temperature is at fever point and I don't know what is wrong with her. *I honestly don't know!*'

She reached out in a a gesture of sympathy and patted Patrick's hand.

'Who's with her now?'

'Molly is there.'

Wearily he shook his head.

'I can't seem to get her temperature down. Sarah is in great discomfort. All night long we've been applying cold compresses but it's been of no use.'

He shrugged his shoulders.

'I'm beaten, Aunt Hetty. Dicky-Sam has gone to Doctor Duncan's house to see if he can spare me a visit.'

'Then all will be well, lad. Sometimes, when we are very close to a person, it is hard to see what's there before our eyes.'

'Perhaps you are right, Aunt,' Patrick conceded, his thoughts a little calmer, 'but soon I must talk to you. My mind is in such a turmoil. I am being pulled all ways . . .'

'And what do you think is causing all this upset, boy?'

Patrick smiled grimly.

'I am, Aunt. I'm reaping the rewards of my own stupidity. I went to London; I know now that I did the wrong thing and there's no way out for me that I can see.'

'Weren't you content in London, then?'

'I thought I was. I thought it was all I could ever want. If I hadn't decided to pay you and Adam a visit I suppose I'd have gone on quite happily working in Harley Street – marrying Arabella. But that's not enough, now. I want to work here, at *The Haven*.'

'Seems you want things all ways, Patrick, and that never makes for an easy solution.'

'I know. I've got myself into a bonny mess.'

'And what of Arabella? Was that her I heard leaving?'

'It was,' Patrick retorted, tersely.

'Was there an upset between you?' Hetty Norris asked anxiously. 'Did you have words?'

'No, not really. Arabella said she couldn't stay at *The Haven* any longer. She wanted me to go back to London with her.'

'And that was all? You're sure there wasn't anything else?'

Patrick straightened himself in his chair, something in his aunt's persistence ringing a small alarm in his mind.

'There was nothing else, Aunt – why do you ask? Should there be anything?'

Hetty Norris looked down at her tightly clenched fingers.

'I don't know, Patrick,' she prevaricated.

'Then what is the point in all these questions?' he persisted. 'What is wrong, Aunt Hetty? What are you trying to say?'

'I suppose I'm trying to tell you that I've been a foolish old woman. I've got myself into a pretty tangle as well as you. Perhaps, you see, it's what I told Arabella last night that made her go off to London.'

Mystified, Patrick did not speak, the sight of the anxious face before him warning him to tread carefully.

'I shouldn't have said what I did, Patrick. I'll never

know what made me do it. It wasn't right to tell her, I know that now.'

'What wasn't right?' Patrick whispered gently.

'It was after Sarah was taken bad. Arabella came in with my supper and I knew there was something troubling the lass. She talked about you – asked what you were like when you were a little boy. I think she wanted to say something. I couldn't find out what it was but she was uneasy and troubled.'

Something inside Patrick's brain clicked sharply into place.

'And what was it you told Arabella?' he prompted, his voice calm and soft.

There was a sharp tip-tapping in the passage outside and an urgent knocking on the bedroom door.

'Damn!' Patrick swore softly, jerking automatically to his feet.

'Be you in there, doctor?' Dicky-Sam called.

Swiftly Patrick opened the door.

'It's Doctor Duncan's carriage – just pulled up outside, sir.'

In an instant Patrick was gone from the room, his eager footsteps seeming almost to run down the stairs.

Hetty Norris lay back on her pillows, sighing with relief that the moment of truth had been postponed. But she would have to tell Patrick. He'd have to understand that she hadn't meant any harm in the telling of it. She'd been proud, in fact. She hoped that Patrick and Arabella had parted without anger. She would never forgive herself she thought sadly, if she had been the cause of Arabella's return to London.

'Lordy,' she whispered, 'but it's a funny old world and no mistake.'

'Sir, I am most grateful that you have come!'

Patrick held out his hand.

Carefully Doctor Duncan laid his top hat and gloves on the empty bench then looked long at the anxious face before him.

'Young Norris, isn't it? Patrick Norris?'

'Yes sir. I attended your lectures when I was apprenticed in Liverpool.'

'Ah, yes,' the older man nodded. 'I mind you well now and young Carmichael. Sad business that, very sad.'

For a moment the elderly Scotsman stood remembering then squared his shoulders and said briskly, 'I take it you want a second opinion, Doctor Norris?'

'Well, sir, not exactly,' Patrick mumbled, suddenly a student again. 'I am not able to diagnose Miss Rigby's illness at all.'

'I see. Then perhaps I can enlighten you, laddie.'

'I'd be most grateful . . .'

Patrick's mouth had suddenly gone dry.

' . . . if you'd come with me, sir –'

He threw open the door of the ward, indicating the screened bed where Sarah lay.

Molly rose to her feet.

'There's no change,' she whispered. 'The poor dear is rambling again and I can't make sense out of any of it!'

Patrick looked with compassion at the burning face that moved restlessly on the pillow and the dry, cracked lips that whispered endlessly in delirium.

'Miss Rigby has sudden surges of high temperature,' he said, 'followed by –'

Doctor Duncan held up his hand.

'Whisht!' he commanded, taking Sarah's hand in his, feeling the erratic pulsebeat with gentle fingertips.

'It's a sorry state ye've got into, Mistress Rigby,' he

smiled. 'Let's see what's to be done with ye, eh?'

Now Patrick felt relief that he was no longer helpless and alone. Beside him was his old tutor, learned and wise. If anyone could help Sarah, it would be he.

All was still in the sick-ward; so still that Patrick fancied his heart thudded loud enough for all to hear. He licked his dry lips, his eyes not leaving the old doctor's face, willing him to come to a decision – a merciful decision.

The long windows were open to the garden yet scarcely a breath of air penetrated the room. Outside, the day had dawned with an eerie yellow light and sullen, heavy clouds hung threatingly low. Perhaps it would rain at last, thought Patrick with an uplifting of hope; perhaps after all it was going to be a good day.

Trying to steady himself, to quieten the heaviness of his anxious heart, Patrick prayed as he had never prayed in his life before.

Let her be well? Only let her get well and I will ask no more of life . . .

Had he known how he would have conjured up the devil himself and struck a bargain there and then – his life, for Sarah's.

The seconds ticked swiftly into an eternity and the old Scottish doctor peered and poked and examined.

'H'mm,' he whispered, and 'Ah-ah,' as though he and Sarah were alone in the room.

Presently he straightened his back and nodded his thanks to Molly.

Patrick's throat was tight, his mouth parched. Hopefully he glanced at Doctor Duncan but read nothing in the face that was blank as a stone slab.

'I'd be obliged, Doctor Norris,' he said quietly, 'if ye would step outside with me.'

From the distance, thunder growled nearer. Inside, the strange yellow light cast an unreal glow on the empty, echoing hall. It seemed that the whole world was waiting with Patrick for what was to come.

The click of the sneck on the ward door vibrated like the crack of a pistol-shot through his brain. He heard himself asking – begging – in a strange, distorted voice, 'What is it, sir? Will she be all right?'

Doctor Duncan picked up his hat and walked unspeaking towards the front door.

Patrick swallowed hard and the action hurt his throat.

'Sir?' he pleaded, trying to control the feeling inside him that made him want to puke with fear.

The older man turned in the doorway, his face still a mask. Then he took a long breath.

'It surprises me, Doctor Norris,' he said, biting off each carefully enunciated word, 'that I should have once thought you had the makings of a fine physician!'

'I'm sorry – I don't understand . . .'

'Once upon a time, laddie, when yourself and Adam Carmichael attended my lectures I had the notion you were an arrogant young puppy but I put up with your daft ways because I had great hopes of you. In my stupidity I even hoped you might stay in Liverpool but to my sorrow you went to London.'

Glowering, he picked up his bag.

'Now, Doctor Norris, I could find it inside me to be glad that you did!'

Patrick had heard the clipped sarcasm many times before but he had never been so surely trounced in all his years as an apprentice.

'Sir,' he stammered, 'if I have called you needlessly I apologize but I still don't know what is wrong with Miss Rigby.'

'Then away back to her bedside and look into her mouth for little white spots and examine the backs of her ears for little red ones!'

'*Measles?*'

'Aye, Doctor Norris. Measles!'

'But she is so ill – her temperature, her delirium –'

Doctor Duncan shook his head wearily.

'The spots will show soon on the abdomen – the fever will quickly abate after that. Measles, in case you have chosen to forget what I tried to teach you, is a childish ailment and thrown off in most cases with impunity. But with an adult, and one who drives herself as Miss Rigby does, it is often a much more distressing matter.'

Then the dour face creased into a rare smile.

'So ye can stop acting like an anxious husband and let me be about my business. By the bye,' he added softly, 'I'd be willing to take back my past comments if I thought you might consider staying with us in Liverpool. Measles apart, young Norris, our need of you is great.'

'There is nothing I want more, sir, but it isn't possible. Now I know Miss Rigby can soon be safely left I must go to London and explain myself.'

'Your employer will not release you?'

'I fear not,' Patrick whispered sadly. 'It seems *The Haven* must close.'

Then as they stood there the little miracle happened and the rain began to fall. It came reluctantly at first making dark grey circles the size of halfpennies on the dust-dry pavement.

Then as the thunder rumbled ever nearer the storm-clouds let loose their precious burden and soon the road outside danced with raindrops.

'My, but that's a rare sight,' Doctor Duncan beamed.

'My, but it's bonny to look at. Now, ye may be sure, the cholera will soon be at an end.'

Rarely, thought Patrick, had he seen his old tutor so elated. Indeed, the sight of the road awash with the longed-for rain must have cheered him into making the offer of help.

'It seems wrong that this house should have to close its doors; there might yet be a way,' he acknowledged, cautiously. 'Perhaps for a while I might be able to loan ye a couple of students. The experience will be good for them and who knows, laddie, your employer down in London just might be more generous than you think, eh?'

So Patrick had accepted the well-meant offer, realizing that as he did so his last excuse for remaining in Liverpool had gone.

Doctor Duncan would ensure that the sick at *The Haven* would be cared for and Sarah was going to get well. It seemed that the Fates that had thrown the two of them together were now conspiring with capricious glee to tear them apart for ever.

Patrick held out his hand.

'I am grateful for all you have done to help us.'

The old doctor turned up the collar of his coat then grasped Patrick's hand firmly.

'Goodbye, laddie. I hope with all my poor heart that all goes well with you in London.'

Then amidst the clatter of horses' hoofs and a cascading of water from the carriage wheels, he was gone.

Patrick stood for a moment, breathing great gulps of cool, moist air into his lungs.

Now he must return to Harley Street. It would be no trouble, he reasoned. He need only acquaint the medical apprentices with their duties at *The Haven*, bid goodbye to his aunt and to Sarah, Molly and Dicky-Sam. Then he would take a ticket for London – it would be as simple and as easy as that.

But when he was in London, how would he fare with half of him still at *The Haven*? How did a man exist when his heart was elsewhere and his body ached with an impossible love?

'Sarah,' he whispered to the grey, uncaring skies. 'Oh Sarah, my dearest love . . .'

Eleven

Patrick placed his tall hat on the seat beside him and stretched out his legs, leaning back his head and closing his eyes, grateful that now he need not move one weary limb until the train stopped in London.

Three weeks ago he had left Harley Street, yet in that brief time he had lived a lifetime and learned a lifetime's wisdom.

He was no longer the self-possessed young physician complacently bound for a holiday in Harrogate. The man who surrendered himself to the rhythmic swaying of the train was another creature, a man who had learned humility, who had glimpsed his guiding star, sadly and too late.

The most he could hope for would be the granting of a few precious days in which to return to *The Haven* and do those things he had promised would be done.

Remember your promise, Patrick? Take care of Sarah for me? Take care of them all . . .?

Still Patrick heard the pathetic plea. He would hear it in every springtime and it would be borne to him on every gentle breeze. In the blaze of summer or the falling of a snowflake Adam's words would come to him. He would never want to forget them, or Sarah.

Sarah was part of him now. She was in his heart and in his mind and whilst his body still ached from wanting her, he knew he would honour his pledge and marry Arabella.

In time it might be easier for him to live with the certain knowledge that Sarah had loved only Adam. It might even become bearable. For Arabella's sake, he hoped it would.

You are a cheat, Patrick Norris, his conscience whispered. He knew now that even his name was a sham. *Norris.* Aunt Hetty's name; the one he had taken for his own; the one he would give to Arabella. Once, it had been important for him to know about his parents. In his early youth he was sure that his pedigree was long and noble, even though lacking the church's blessing.

'There's things you must know now that you're going back to London and they'll not keep any longer,' his aunt said as he sat by her bedside only that morning. 'I told Arabella, Patrick, and now I've got to tell you.'

'Well, Aunt,' he had gently asked. 'What did you tell Arabella?'

'I told her who you were and where you came from.'

'I see.'

The calmness of Patrick's voice seemed to take Hetty Norris aback and for a time there was silence in the little room. Then, unable to contain herself any longer she demanded,

'Well – ask me then – you've been trying to ferret it out of me for years! Ask me who your mother was!'

His mother? Strange, thought Patrick, he'd managed all his life without one. Aunt Hetty had been all he'd needed, truth known. Did it really matter who that unknown woman was? Could his flesh-and-blood mother have done more for him than Hetty Norris had done? Were there not more important things to be worried about, now?

'Very well, Aunt, I will ask you who my mother was but at this moment I care precious little, I am so tired.'

'You . . . *what*?'

'It doesn't seem to matter so much, now. It is more important that I should try to straighten myself out, think about my future – not worry over what is past.'

A smile of love and pride gentled the old face.

'Then I will tell you, boy, and gladly, because I reckon now you've grown up enough to be told!'

Taking his hands in hers she said quietly,

'Strange, for it's like giving my own son away . . .'

'Who am I, Aunt Het?' Patrick whispered.

'That I don't rightly know, Patrick. You see, I found you on the doorstep.'

'*Abandoned*, you mean?'

'Aye lad, by some desperate woman or a poor unwed lass, perhaps. All I knew about you was your name. It was pinned to your blanket – just that and the date of your birth.'

Patrick gave a small, mirthless laugh.

'You know, I don't know why, but I thought I was the love-child of some rich young lady. Sometimes, you see, I seemed to remember a large house and lofty rooms and rows of bobbing bells.'

'Aye, Patrick, you'd remember all that for you were left on the doorstep of my master's house. His three daughters took a liking to you and so did I. That's why my master let me keep you, provided you stayed below stairs with the servants.'

'But you supported me all my life? I had thought it must have been my mother's family or my natural father.'

'No, lad. My master and mistress left Liverpool shortly after that so I stayed behind and took the little house in Lace Street. I scrubbed and did washing to support us.

You've been the son I never had. I've been proud of you – so very proud.'

'But my education, Aunt Hetty? Did you pay for that as well? Did Black Becky bleed you dry so that your little foundling might have his chance in life?'

Hetty Norris's eyes filled with tears.

'I didn't want you to find out about that, but I had to go to Becky Solomon. It was the only way I could come by so much money. I'm sorry . . .'

'*Sorry?* It is I who am sorry, for my stupid pride!'

He fished eagerly in his pocket-book and took out the almost-forgotten receipt.

'Here,' he said, placing the paper in her hand, 'a present for you.'

Hetty Norris frowned.

'You know I can't read. What does it say?'

'It says you are out of Rebecca Solomon's debt for all time.'

'Oh, bless you, lad,' the old woman whispered. 'I've been fair worried lying here, thinking about the tally-man.'

Patrick reached out for her, holding her close, placing his cheek to hers.

'I was a child of the streets, Aunt, unloved and un-wanted –'

For just a little time a feeling of indescribable sadness possessed him.

'No, boy, that's not true. You *were* wanted. *I* wanted you the minute I set eyes on you, and maybe your real mother loved you more than I did. Like as not she loved you too much to keep you. One day you'll understand what I mean by that.'

Then she placed her hands on his shoulders and held him at arm's length, looking into his eyes as she spoke.

'You know, deep down inside her, every woman wants a child in her arms. Like as not it doesn't matter how she gets it or even who fathers it. You have been *my* son, Patrick. You weren't of my body but you were the child of my heart.'

Her eyes misted with tears again and she could not hide the tremble in her voice as she whispered,

'Don't think too badly of your mother, Patrick. It must have been terrible to have to give you away. She left you at the bottom of the steps that led off the street and down to the kitchens. Like as not she thought you'd find more compassion there than there'd be at the front door.'

Hetty Norris sighed, remembering.

'But my master and mistress were good people. They didn't have you sent away. They could have given you to the *Ladies' Charity*. The *Charity* would have found some place for you – they'd not have put you in the workhouse – but it's hard for waifs, at times. Sometimes the wrong people get hold of them and they're often put upon – worked hard and cruelly used. I couldn't have risked that happening to you, boy.'

The old eyes pleaded for understanding. It was almost as if they were asking that he should forgive her for withholding the truth for so long.

'Oh you dear, stupid, wonderful old lady!' Patrick exulted. 'What can I say to you? I can only thank God that my mother, who ever she was, had the good sense to leave me on *your* doorstep!'

Then they were laughing and crying at one and the same time and Patrick's heart was suddenly a little less sad.

'Now, boy, we must talk seriously. Just what are your intentions, might I ask?'

'With regard to *The Haven*, you mean?'

'Aye, and to Arabella and your position in London. You've got to get yourself sorted out.'

'How did Arabella take it, Aunt, learning I was a nobody, I mean?'

'She took it very well. It seemed to me that it made very little difference at all. She had other things on her mind, if you ask me.'

'I haven't treated her very kindly, have I?'

Hetty Norris shrugged.

'Perhaps not, but maybe it's been good for the lass to stay at *The Haven*. It might have helped her to see the other side of life. She'll be all the better a wife for you, for the knowing.'

If you're still bent on marrying her. If you really loved her, Patrick . . .

'Look, lad,' she said when Patrick remained silent. 'I've tried to rear you to respect the truth and to act with honour. You've got a duty to your employer and to that poor girl. There's nobody can sort out your life now, but yourself.'

'I know,' Patrick shook his head miserably. 'I want so much to stay in Liverpool as Adam always wanted I should. But would Doctor Harrington release me and would Arabella live here?'

'I don't know, Patrick. I'd like you to come home but it's something you've got to work out for yourself. You'll do what's right, I know it.'

Aye, her mind supplied, *you'll stay with Doctor Harrington and you'll wed his daughter because I've brought you up to honour your word.*

'Yes, Aunt. I shall do what is right, I promise you.'

He had given her hand a little squeeze then, as he rose to take his leave of her.

'Thank you, dear Mother Hetty. Thank you for everything.'

Patrick Norris. Patrick Nobody.

The words chased round and round in his head. Funny, but he didn't care now; he really didn't care. In a strange way he was almost glad. He was a foundling. He had been spewed up by the Liverpool gutters and he wanted to return to the people who lived there – his own people. He needed them as much as they needed him.

Carefully he pushed tobacco into his pipe, staring unseeing from the window of the compartment, realizing that every second was taking him further away from Sarah.

He smiled gently as he recalled their goodbye. She had been sitting up in bed, her long hair tied back with a ribbon, her face covered with tiny bright-red spots.

'You look like a little girl,' he teased, desperately trying to make their moment of parting easier for himself.

'I don't feel like a little girl. I just want to stay here and sleep and sleep. Aren't I wicked?'

'Oh, very wicked and slothful, Sarah Rigby,' he smiled, wishing with all his heart that he too might be allowed to sleep for a week.

'Doctor Duncan's apprentices seem very keen to do their best to help,' Sarah said. 'I wish Adam could have employed students. We thought about it often and decided we couldn't afford even one.'

She smiled, ruefully.

'They eat so much, don't they, young growing men?'

They were making small-talk, Patrick had realized. Best he should get it over with as soon as he could.

'I must go now,' he said, tersely, 'but I will be back, Sarah, even if it is only for a few days. I must write again to Adam's parents and send them his personal things.'

'Yes, Patrick,' Sarah whispered. Then she smiled.

'I'm sure we shall be all right. You must not worry about us. Doctor Duncan has promised to look in, hasn't he, from time to time?'

Patrick nodded.

'Goodbye then, Sarah,' he said briefly. 'Take care of yourself.'

He strode from the ward without giving her his hand or permitting himself even one small backward glance, his body trembling with the effort of self-control. He had wanted to grasp her in his arms and hold her close; tell her that when he came back nothing would keep him from her ever again. He would have given a great deal to have been able to say that.

Dearest Sarah, his heart yearned. *Gentle, proud, beautiful Sarah. I know so little about you yet I love you so much.*

. . . so much; so much; so much; echoed the wheels of the train that carried him so relentlessly nearer to London.

The street lamps shone brightly as Patrick's cab swung smoothly out of Wimpole Street and into Harley Street, but for the first time Patrick felt no burst of elation as he drove down that famous road; only a feeling of guilt that was mingled with sorrow and regret.

The front door of Doctor Harrington's house was opened to him before he had scarcely had time to pull the bell. It was as if someone had been waiting breathlessly for his return.

Arabella ran lightly down the thickly-carpeted stairs as

Patrick handed his hat and gloves to the primly starched housemaid. Somewhere, it was certain, the footman would already be attending to his baggage.

For a moment Arabella and Patrick hesitated, strangely shy, each eyeing the other for some small sign of what was to come. Then Arabella held out her hands.

'My dear,' she whispered, softly.

Patrick bent to kiss her cheek, feeling a strange relief that the first awkward moments of their meeting seemed not to be tainted with the promise of bitterness.

'Did you have a good journey?'

'Yes, I thank you. The train made splendid time.'

Now they were talking to each other quite calmly, acting like distant cousins, polite and affectionate.

Arabella linked her arm through Patrick's, walking beside him to the first-floor drawing-room.

'I am glad to have this time alone with you, Patrick, but we may not have long. Papa is at the opera and will soon be home. Before he comes there is something I must say to you. It is important to both of us that you should know what it is before you speak to my father.'

Patrick frowned.

'It sounds very mysterious, Arabella.'

'Not really,' she shook her head, 'but I have told papa about *The Haven* and the conditions there. I think I might have helped a little. At least he understands now why you needed to be so long away.'

Patrick felt an unaccustomed surge of gratitude towards Arabella. He was amazed to see such a subtle change in her.

Now she no longer wore her hair in fashionable ringlets but had swept it into a chignon in the nape of her neck as Sarah did. There was a new maturity about her too, and an air of calmness.

Patrick lowered his tired body into a chair and closed his eyes, trying to shut Arabella out, to see instead Sarah's beloved face. But the lamps glowed softly, the chair cushioned him gently and try as he might that loved face eluded him in the richness and comfort of the room. Yet somewhere in the misty distance, tiny alms-houses stood by a cemetery and a gentle voice sighed insistent into the summer dusk,

'Take care of Sarah for me, Patrick? Take care of them all . . .'

Excitedly, Kate Tarleton burst into the kitchen.

'It's here, Miss Rigby! The waggon's come!'

Sarah set down the apple she was peeling.

'Very well, Kate,' she smiled, wondering afresh at the exuberance of the very young, for little more than two weeks ago Kate had lain bruised and bleeding, the cause and the victim of a brothel fight.

Now, her cheeks plump and rosy again, she had waited eagerly since sun-up for the arrival of the farm cart that was to carry her, along with Margaret-Mary Haggarty and her family, to the sweet, rich farmlands beyond Ormskirk. She was dancing with impatience at the head of the stone steps when the driver pulled the great Clydesdale stallion to a halt outside *The Haven*, and flinging her arms around Sarah's neck she kissed her cheek affectionately.

'God bless you, Miss, for what you and Doctor Patrick have done for me. I'll never forget you both, not ever!' she vowed fervently.

Sarah hugged Kate close, sorry that the lovable girl was leaving, yet glad she would now have a good home and a kindly mistress.

'Be off with you child,' she said, her voice husky with emotion and in an instant Kate was perched alongside the waggoner, her young face glowing with pure joy.

Sarah held up her hand to Margaret-Mary Haggarty who sat atop the waggon with her sparse belongings and her many children.

''Tis sorry I am not to be seein' Doctor Patrick for don't I owe my life to the dear man?' she whispered to Sarah. 'I'd have liked fine to show him his namesake,' she said proudly, looking down at the sleeping boy-child who had been born against the most fearful of odds.

Patrick had been magnificent that day, Sarah remembered. She had been proud to work by his side. She thought, too, of the night they had gone together to the tavern in Leather Lane and the compassion Patrick had shown for Kate, little more than a child yet forced into prostitution that she might exist. Now Kate would never need to go back to the Liverpool streets.

There was so much goodness still in the world, Sarah thought as she waved goodbye to the waggon-load of happiness. Now the Haggartys and Kate Tarleton were beginning a new life in the peace of the countryside, the heartbreaking circumstances of their old lives behind them.

Sarah thought with gratitude of the promptness with which the friend of her schooldays had answered her plea for help, offering a farm cottage to Margaret-Mary in exchange for sewing-work, and the job of dairymaid to Kate. Now, as the waggon rumbled out of the square, Sarah turned once more to *The Haven*, trying desperately to ignore the fact that slowly and surely it was becoming an empty, silent shell.

George and Tilly Hanson and little Ben had already left for Macclesfield at the promise of regular work in the silk mills there and now Kate had gone.

The sick-ward was almost empty and the dispensary almost bare of medicines and drugs for it was another week before the *Bounty* was due. Almost all the food Patrick had bought was gone too and there was no money left with which to buy more. Soon the medical apprentices would return to Doctor Duncan and the doors of *The Haven* would finally close. Then there would be just the three of them; Molly, Dicky-Sam and herself to remember the good days when Adam had been alive and hope had run high.

Slowly Sarah walked down to the kitchens, wondering yet again how Patrick was faring and how much longer she would have to wait before there was news of him from London.

It was strange, she mused, that she had not liked Patrick when first they met yet now she found herself starting hopefully at the sound of an approaching cab or a sudden knocking on the front door.

But Patrick too had gone and with him all hopes that *The Haven* could continue for Sarah knew how difficult it would be for him to return, even for the few days he had hoped to be given.

' . . . and I'll tell ye, Dicky-Sam Pickstock, that there's not much time left for us all at *The Haven*.'

Molly's voice floated disconsolately from the kitchen.

'I'm thinking the landlord will be setting the bailiffs on us now that Doctor Adam's gone, God-rest-him.'

'No, Molly, the landlord won't do that,' Sarah spoke quietly from the kitchen doorway. 'At least I can promise you both that we shall have a roof over our heads until we can decide what is to be done.'

'But how can ye be so sure?' Molly demanded, doubtfully.

'Because *The Haven* belongs to me.'

'To *you*, Miss Sarah?'

Molly's teacup dropped with a clatter.

'You mean that it's been yourself that hasn't taken a penny rent all these years?'

'Yes,' Sarah nodded. 'I am the mysterious landlord and Adam never knew,' she whispered, sadly.

'And the *Bounty*, miss?' Dicky-Sam asked. 'Has that been of your sending, an' all?'

'It is sent by the notaries of my late aunt. She left me shares that allow me an income of five guineas a month. That, and this house is all I have, but I wanted to give it to Adam to help run *The Haven*. To have it sent secretly was the only way I could find to make him accept it.'

Sarah shrugged her shoulders, anticipating Molly's next question.

'Don't talk about it any more, Molly, there's a dear soul. I'll tell you – in my own good time – I promise. But not now . . .'

'Why, to be sure, Miss Sarah,' Molly retorted, blushing to the roots of her hair, 'such a thing never entered me head, so it didn't, but you'll be fine, now. You'll be able to sell this great barn of a place and find a nice snug little house, somewhere.'

'No, Molly, I want us all to stay together. I promised Doctor Adam it would be like that. We'll manage, the three of us.'

She tilted her chin and smiled.

'Why, who knows, perhaps even now Doctor Patrick is on his way back to us!'

Dicky-Sam and Molly nodded but their eyes were empty of hope. They knew as well as Sarah knew that Patrick had been gone for almost a week and time was running out.

Sarah rose abruptly to her feet.

'Will you give Miss Hetty her breakfast then help her to dress, Molly? I am going out for a little while.'

'But, Miss Sarah, you've not long been out of your sickbed,' Molly protested. 'Let Dicky-Sam go with you?'

'No, Molly; you are kind and I thank you, but I must go alone.'

The kitchen door closed behind Sarah and Dicky-Sam shook his head sadly.

'Poor lass,' he said softly.

'Oh? And why do you say that, Dicky-Sam Pickstock,' Molly demanded. 'And why is herself the owner of a house such as this yet as poor as a churchmouse, God love her?'

Carefully avoiding the little man's eyes she filled her teacup afresh.

'Not that it's any concern of mine, mark ye. Never let it be said that Molly O'Keefe's a busy-body . . .'

She shrugged her shoulders and pulled up a chair to the table.

' . . . And another thing,' she continued, now in full spate, 'where's the girl going that's so secret we can't be told? Will ye tell me that, Dicky?'

'Aye, I'll tell ye for I'll wager a year's pay I know where she's a'going.'

He paused, dramatically, savouring his moment of importance.

'They're going to sink the *Cornucopia* this forenoon, aren't they?'

'They are, too, and a good riddance to the evil ship, says I.'

'Well, don't you see, Molly? Reckon Miss Sarah's going to be there to see the last of the packet.'

Molly shrugged her shoulders doubtfully.

'And why should she want to do that?'

'Eh, woman, don't you understand? If Miss Sarah owns this house then she's old Mad Jonathan's kin, ain't she? Like as not Miss Sarah once owned that jonah-ship!'

'I'll not believe that!'

'Then believe what you want, Molly O'Keefe. You've not lived in Liverpool all your days like I have. I was a seaman remember afore I was nearly killed on the *Cornucopia*. I knows all about Liverpool ships and ship-owners.'

'Then who was Mad Jonathan, will ye tell me?'

'He was Jonathan Rigby, a shipowner. He was all respectable on top, but there's some as knew all along where he got his money from. It came from slaving, Molly, and that's a fact!'

'God help us! Tainted money!'

'Aye, and old Jonathan made sure his wealth stayed in the Rigby family. He only had one child – a daughter he called Sarah and he married this Sarah off to her cousin – name of Rigby, too. That way he kept an eye on his investments, see? Well, talk had it that this daughter and her new husband made a sea journey on the *Cornucopia* and they never came back; died at sea, both of 'em and buried at sea, an' all. They left a child behind them, little more'n a babe and that little lass was our Miss Sarah, like as not. I don't know what become of that little one. Folks said she was packed off to some school in the south as soon as she was old enough. Old Jonathan couldn't stand the sight of the poor little thing – reminded him over much of his dead daughter.'

'Poor lonely little wench,' Molly sniffed. 'Poor Miss Sarah.'

'Aye, I reckon old Jonathan Rigby took a turn for the worse when that ship docked and the Master had to break the news to him. Stood on the quayside and cursed something awful, he did. Then he cursed the ship, an'all and had her name changed, there and then. He'd called that ship for his daughter, see? That slave-ship was once called the *Sarah*. Funny, I've known that all along but I never connected old Mad Jonathan and his packet with *our* Miss Sarah.'

He shook his head sadly.

'Changing a ship's name ain't good you know. Calling her the *Cornucopia* was bound to bring ill-luck, I'm thinking.'

'And this ship's Master? What happened to him, then?'

'Don't know, Molly. Didn't even know his name. You see, I didn't sail on the *Cornucopia* until she changed hands; she had a different Master, then; one as kept his mouth shut tight, an' all.'

'But I thought shipowners were rich, grand folk, Dicky,' Molly hazarded, doubtfully. 'Poor Miss Sarah ain't rich.'

'No, she's not and that's a fact. Old Jonathan went from bad to worse. Died of drink, in the end, in a dock-side gutter. They said he left nothing but a pile of debts and the *Cornucopia*. All his money went on cards and dicing and drinking. You see, they'd stopped slaving by that time. There was no more money coming in. Jonathan Rigby wasn't a good merchant. All he dealt in or knew anything about, for that matter, was black ivory – slaves.'

Molly carried the cups to the sinkstone.

'Poor Miss Sarah. No wonder she feared that ship. And she'd be mortal shocked I'll not doubt, when she found out where the money came from that paid for her fine upbringing. Imagine the shame of slave-trading? And 'twas the *Cornucopia* sick that brought cholera into this house, never forget that,' she whispered, sadly.

'Aye, Molly and maybe it would be as well if *The Haven* was to close its doors. Miss Sarah has worked herself to a shadow here and it's my belief she's done it on account of being a Rigby, I'm thinking. She's ashamed of her past kin and being reared on bad money. She's been trying to even things up, if you ask me.'

But for once, Molly O'Keefe had nothing to say. She turned her back on Dicky-Sam and busied herself with the washing of the breakfast crocks. She wished he'd take himself off to the market. Molly O'Keefe wanted to be alone; she wanted to weep for Miss Sarah and poor young Doctor Adam. She wanted to weep until she was sick for the wickedness of the world ...

Sarah sat down on a hummock of grass, surprised that she felt so tired but realizing it was important that she should come to the jutting arm of land that reached far out into the wide River Mersey. People called it the Wishing Gate and today Sarah would wait with other women who kept vigil there and bid farewell to a part of her life.

Women who waited at the Wishing Gate were often seen to weep for there they watched the passing of the ships that bore their men away and they wished them God-speed and a safe landfall, standing there until the mast-tops had merged into the distant horizon where the river poured itself into the sea.

Sarah waited too for the passing of a ship. She awaited the jonah-ship, the condemned *Cornucopia*. The packet was old and unsafe and her timbers rotten. She had housed cholera victims, tied up there in the middle of the river, and no mount of limewashing would ever cleanse her of the disease. Now the Port Authority had demanded that she be packed with explosives and floated down-river to the open sea, there to be sunk. It gave Sarah a strange satisfaction to know that soon all the ill-luck and evil the ship had attracted to itself would be gone for ever. Perhaps, with the sinking of the *Cornucopia*, everything would come right.

So much was going out of her life, Sarah thought. Since she could remember, she had been lonely; it seemed that Fate had decreed it should be so. Dear, gentle Adam was gone and still she had not wept for him for her grief was too fierce for tears.

Now Patrick had left, taking with him that feeling of safeness she had come almost to depend upon. If only he had been able to stay at *The Haven*, she yearned, and take up where Adam had left off. Patrick was such a fine doctor, Sarah thought sadly; so skilful and confident. What could they not have accomplished, he and Adam, at the house in Abercromby Square?

Sarah hugged her shawl around her, straining her eyes for signs of the Cornucopia's approach. She would know that ship at once, even from a distance. She would sense its coming, that ship that had once been named the *Sarah*. She knew every mast and spar, every inch of rigging.

'Dear God,' she prayed, silently, 'will I never be free of the curse of my forebears? Shall I ever rid myself of the shame of it all?'

How could her grandfather have done it? How could he have sold his fellow-creatures like dumb beasts? Surely that was the devil's work, she thought, grateful that now men could no longer live by such evil.

A rough but kindly voice pulled Sarah's thoughts away from the past.

'Are you all right, lass? Trembling something awful, you are.'

'Thank you, ma'am, but I am only a little cold. I have not been well —'

Her voice trailed away as the *Cornucopia* hove into sight.

The packet's sails were tightly furled and lashed; her masts, yards and bowsprit sticking out like skeletal fingers as two of the new steam-tugs, importantly belching coal-smoke, nosed and fussed her down-river. And as the ship a madman once cursed went slowly to her destruction, the woman with the sad grey eyes who stood at the Wishing Gate said goodbye to so much of the unhappiness in her past life.

With her solemn passing, the *Cornucopia* took with her a mother and father Sarah had never known, an old man driven mad by misery and remorse, the bewildered crying of poor negro souls and the soft sad sighing of a gentle young doctor.

'May God forgive the evil you have had a part in,' Sarah whispered to the ship that would soon lie in a million pieces beneath the sea. 'May I live long enough to right some of the wrongs those before me have caused.'

If only there could be a way, she wished desperately, to keep *The Haven* open. For Adam's sake she must try. Adam's sacrifice must not be allowed to have been made in vain. She would remember the promise she made to him; keep his face before her as a talisman.

'Oh, Adam, my dear,' she whispered.

Then the tears she had denied for so long began to fall and she sat with the arms of the kindly stranger around her and wept for Adam until she could weep no more.

'There now,' soothed the woman, her rough hand

gently stroking Sarah's hair. 'There now, lass, stop your weeping. He'll soon be back.'

But you don't understand, Sarah thought desperately. *He won't be back. He's never coming back!*

Twelve

Sarah walked slowly homeward, looking across the fields at the end of Vauxhall Road to the slowly-turning sails of the tall windmill, remembering clearly the day Great-aunt Polly had said,

'Well, he's dead at last. You'll have to know now, for you've inherited a fair load of trouble, Sarah girl!'

Sarah had been just seventeen then and old Polly Rigby had only two years left to live, had they known it. She had been happy in the little house set deep in the Cheshire countryside; glad to be rid of the select boarding establishment for young ladies and live in a real home at last. She hadn't known a great deal about her parents except that they had died young within two days of each other and had been consigned to the waters that washed the African shores. It was a mysterious ailment, Aunt Polly said and tight-lipped had left it at that.

Then *He* had died and Sarah came to know of the existence of Mad Jonathan – Jonathan Septimus Rigby, her grandfather.

'Why didn't you tell me, Aunt Polly? I didn't know that all this time I had a grandfather.'

'Best you shouldn't know until you had to, girl.'

'But he's dead now and I'll never know him. I'd have liked to have known him – talked to him about my parents, about my mother . . .'

'That you wouldn't! The mention of your mother's name would have set him ranting like the mad creature he was. And he wouldn't have you near him; he said so, the day the *Sarah* docked and they told him your mother was dead. Jonathan Rigby was twisted with hatred; he was rotten to the core.'

'How can you say that, Aunt Polly? Why are you so bitter, and he your own brother?'

'I didn't own him. Rather to have no one left in the world than to be kin to a slave-trader!'

'A slaver? Oh, no! I won't believe it! I'd have known; I'd have heard about it, somehow . . .'

'No one knew, save a few. I knew it and the Master of the *Sarah* knew it –'

'But no one has ever seen slaves in Liverpool, it's a well-known fact. It must be a lie about my grandfather, it must!'

'It's no lie, Sarah Rigby. There weren't any slaves came into the port but that's not to say slaving didn't go on. No ship's Master ever dared bring blacks into the place. He'd have had them all thrown overboard before he'd have done that. No, my girl. On the surface of it, my brother was a merchant. He loaded his ship with guns and cheap gin and took them to the African coast. The ship's Master traded them for negroes and those poor creatures were shackled like animals in the hold and taken straight to America. They were traded there for cotton and tobacco and molasses and sugar – all very respectable. Everybody knew it went on yet nobody admitted to working the triangular run, as they called it.'

'Dear God,' Sarah whispered. 'My mother, my grandfather – even *you*, Aunt Polly – lived on bad money.'

'Aye, we did and we shall pay for it, just as your grandfather and your mother before you paid for it. Us

Rigbys'll never be free of it, make up your mind to that, Sarah!'

And when it was all over and done with, when the creditors had been paid and the debts settled there was only the re-named *Sarah* left and the empty, neglected house in Abercromby Square.

The *Sarah*, named for her mother and on which her mother had died was sold to continue its evil as the *Cornucopia*, and the house in Abercromby Square had been leased by her notary to a young doctor, a gently-spoken Scotsman named Adam.

That had been little more than six years ago and like Great-aunt Polly, Adam too was dead. It seemed to Sarah that as soon as she learned to love a person she was fated to lose them. Were the Rigbys truly cursed or dare she hope that now the curse lay at the bottom of the sea with the remains of the *Cornucopia*?

She had tried so hard. Surely things would go right, now?

Dicky-Sam was waiting outside the surgery door, a large mug of tea in his hand when Sarah walked wearily into *The Haven*.

'Lord bless us, miss, ye've been away so long I was off to find the Town Crier!'

Sarah smiled at the little man's concern. Dicky-Sam never changed, she thought. No matter what happened, he always made it his duty to take in a mug of tea as the last patient left the surgery.

'I'm sorry I caused you to worry, Dicky,' she said, eyeing the mug longingly. 'Do you think Molly might have any tea left in her pot?'

'To be sure she will, Miss Sarah. If you'd like to take this mug in to the doctor, I'll bring up another for you.'

'Bless you,' smiled Sarah, knocking gently before opening the door of the surgery.

Then she stood transfixed, willing her hands to stop their sudden trembling, holding the mug tightly lest it hurtle to the floor. She took a deep, steadying breath,

'Your tea, doctor,' she smiled, tremulously, not knowing whether to laugh or to cry, wanting desperately to shout with joy at the sight of his face.

He was back! Patrick had come as he said he would! Now she knew, her heart beating joyfully, that she could tell him all her worries and he would help things to come right. Now, for just a little time, she could feel safe again.

Gravely Patrick rose to his feet.

'You are looking much better, Sarah,' he said quietly, willing himself to be calm. 'It is good to see you again.'

'Patrick! It is good to see you, too! How much time do you have? Two days? . . . three? Oh, I have so much to ask you. I need your advice on so many things.'

She perched herself on the edge of the desk, laughing joyfully.

Patrick sat down again, urging himself back to normality, clenching his hands on the arms of his chair so that he might not reach out and touch the cheek flushed pink with excitement.

A pulse beat in his throat at the beauty of her. How wonderful it would be if she could always look at him with eyes that shone like summer sunlight. But she was only relieved to see him, of that he was sure. Women like Sarah only loved once and Adam had been Sarah's man. Patrick knew that all he could have hoped for would have been second-best and that he would never have accepted.

'I will be glad to help you in any way I can, Sarah. I have been giving a great deal of thought to the running of *The Haven* – the two unused bedrooms, for instance.'

Sarah puckered her forehead.

'Yes, Patrick?'

'Hmm. I often felt it was wrong that they should stand empty. Had you never thought of putting them to better use?'

'Yes, of course we had.'

Sarah was completely mystified.

' . . . but we could not afford even to furnish them, let alone run them. Perhaps if we had had apprentices it might have been possible. But why are you saying all this, Patrick? Far from taking on more work, I'm afraid we shall now be able to do very little here, at all.'

Patrick smiled gently.

'But had you not thought,' he persisted, 'that with those two rooms made available, there could be separate wards for men and women and there could be a laying-in room for mothers in labour? Women should not suffer in child-birth. They should have the benefit of chloroform when they are confined. Chloroform has been in use in Edinburgh now for three years and more and more London doctors are acknowledging its great advantages.'

Sarah's head buzzed.

'Stop, Patrick! You know all this is not possible.'

Patrick reached out and took Sarah's hands in his, smiling into her bewildered eyes.

'But it *is* possible, Sarah, and I intend to make it so.'

'How? With the best will in the world, Patrick, I cannot follow your reasoning.'

'We will take an apprentice,' he replied, triumphantly. 'We will take *two*!'

'*We?*'

It cannot be possible, thought Sarah. Patrick cannot be teasing? Surely he couldn't be so cruel?'

'Yes Sarah. *We!*'

Patrick laughed with delight, no longer able to keep the news from her. '*I've come home, to The Haven!*'

'To *stay*?' she whispered, incredulously. 'Oh, I can't believe it. I'm asleep! I am dreaming the loveliest of dreams!'

She turned to Dicky-Sam who stood in the doorway, a mug of steaming tea in his hand.

'You didn't tell me, Dicky!' She was laughing and crying at one and the same time. 'Why didn't you say that Doctor Patrick was back?'

The weatherbeaten face creased into a thousand happy wrinkles.

'Why, Miss Sarah, 'twould have spoiled the surprise, wouldn't it?'

'But he's staying with us. Doctor Patrick isn't going back to London and I can't believe it. It isn't true!'

'Well, if the doctor's only here on a fleeting visit then all I can say, miss, is that we've lugged and tugged an awful lot of baggage up to the attic,' Dicky laughed as he closed the door behind him, leaving them alone again.

'Oh, Patrick, I'm so glad.' Sarah hugged herself with joy, 'but you must have a better room. It would not be proper, when you are married, for Arabella to have to sleep in the attic.'

'Arabella won't be coming to Liverpool, Sarah,' Patrick replied quietly. 'She has released me from our pledge. We are not to be married, now.'

'Oh, Patrick, what can I say?' Sarah whispered. 'I am so sorry. If anything that happened at *The Haven* was the cause of, I shall never forgive myself.'

'Perhaps, indirectly,' Patrick acknowledged, '*The Haven* had something to do with it, but you must not blame yourself, Sarah.'

The Haven, Patrick thought, had just been the start of it. At *The Haven*, both he and Arabella had found themselves, had recognized the selfishness of the lives they had lived, the falseness of the opulent world they had created about themselves.

Patrick smiled. 'Indeed, I have to thank Arabella that Doctor Harrington agreed to release me from my bond. It was she who made her father realize I was needed here; that my heart was here, too.'

'And you?' Sarah whispered. 'How do you feel about it?'

'A little sad,' Patrick acknowledged, 'but glad we found out in time. We were not truly in love, Arabella and I.'

'But your good living at Harley Street? You have given up so much to return to Liverpool.'

Patrick smiled and shook his head.

'No, Sarah. If you knew the truth of it, I shall be the richer by far for coming home.'

He threw back his head and laughed aloud.

'Don't you realize that my roots are here, deep and secure in the back streets of this town? I was an abandoned child – forsaken by my parents. I was a doorstep baby, Sarah, and I am not ashamed of it. I only want to be with my own people. What more is there to ask of life?'

Perhaps only you, Sarah, his heart whispered dully. *Just you, my dear one.*

'And was it because of that – because of your beginnings, I mean – that Arabella decided not to marry you?'

'No, Sarah. I thought at first it might have been the reason, but it wasn't. Strangely enough, it made little difference to her.'

How could he tell Sarah, he thought, what Arabella had really said?

'*I love you, Patrick. In my own way, I love you as much as I am capable of loving any man. But I don't love you enough,*' she had said, '*to give up my life in London and follow you to Liverpool.*'

Arabella had laughed then; a brave, sad little laugh.

'I have persuaded papa, you see, that your future lies in Liverpool and that is true, Patrick, in more ways than one.'

'What do you mean, Arabella?' Patrick had whispered apprehensively.

'Oh, Patrick. If you had once looked at me as you looked at Sarah, I would have followed you to the ends of the earth!'

Arabella had known, he realized dully. All that time it must have been plain for everyone to see. Everyone of course, but Sarah. She had loved Adam . . .

'Then I am glad for you, if you are not unhappy. Do you know,' she laughed, 'I went to the Wishing Gate this morning. How long I was there I don't know – hours and hours, I think – and I made a wish.'

'Yes, Sarah?'

'I wished there could be a way to keep *The Haven* open. In my wildest dreams, I could not have expected it to happen, but it has. You are back!'

So that is all I mean to you, Sarah, Patrick thought, sadly; just a means of keeping *The Haven* open.

But it didn't matter. He was back in Liverpool and there was much to be done. At least he would be near Sarah and he must be content with that. For once in his life he conceded, he must take second-best.

He said, 'I am concerned about Aunt Hetty. Do you think it would be possible for her to remain here? Had I stayed in London I could have afforded to make her a comfortable allowance and she could have returned to Lace Street. But now –' he shrugged.

'But of course she must stay with us, Patrick. She is a dear old lady and she will be most welcome. Already she and Molly are firm friends.'

Relieved, Patrick nodded his thanks.

'There is another thing too, Sarah. The tenancy of this house was in Adam's name, wasn't it?'

Sarah nodded.

'Then before I make any more grand plans, I think it would be wise if I tried to contact the owner of *The Haven*.'

'What good would that do, Patrick?'

Sarah felt a small shiver of fear. If Patrick got in touch with her notaries, the past she wanted so much to live down might become evident. She had managed when Adam was alive to keep it to herself. Perhaps with Patrick it might not be so easy. She didn't want to admit that she was the grand-daughter of the notorious Mad Jonathan; that she had lived in comparative luxury when Patrick had lived in Lace Street.

Now she only wanted to serve humanity; to give back to life a little of what her greedy forebears had wrenched from it.

'Perhaps it would do no good at all, Sarah, but the owner of this house chose not to accept rent from Adam. If I were to ask him for the tenancy, things might take on a very different light. First, I must make sure that we can all remain at *The Haven*.'

'Oh, Patrick, let us not worry today about such things. Tomorrow, as Molly always says, is always the best day to look for trouble!'

Please, begged Sarah silently, *let me not have to tell him just yet who I am?*

'Perhaps you are right, Sarah. Today is special, but tomorrow I must really set to work.'

He laughed, his eyes shining at the thought of each wonderful new day and the challenge it would bring. With the help of apprentices Patrick knew he could take on more patients who were able to pay well for medical treatment. Rich men and women, he reasoned, could help pay for the treatment of the poor ones. He grinned, happily. He'd never before thought of himself as a latter-day Robin Hood.

'I must go out, Sarah, for a little while. I want to see Doctor Duncan and I must call upon the good ladies of the *Charity* and prevail upon their generosity. I need not only apprentices but beds and blankets for our new wards.'

Sarah stood at the surgery window and watched Patrick's jaunty walk and the debonair set of his hat as he set off in search of his old tutor.

Foolish tears of happiness pricked her eyes. There was a warm glow inside her and all around her; the safe-feeling she had never expected to know again.

'Oh, Adam,' she whispered, turning her face upwards, 'Patrick is back. He's home again to take care of your poor ones. It's going to be all right.'

Patrick stood by the moss-covered statue in the tangled garden behind *The Haven* and looked into the gathering dusk of late summer.

The scent of moss roses and honeysuckle was all about him and with it came memories of the first time he stood there, the night he had known the hopeless discovering of his love for Sarah.

Now, in the cool of the rain-washed August gloaming, he felt again that same forlorn desire.

Impatiently he wrenched his thoughts to other things; to the Ladies' Charity who had promised him the beds with which to furnish the new laying-in ward for women in labour and Doctor Duncan who had grasped his hand with nothing short of delight and offered all the apprentices he could use.

Life would not be easy, Patrick acknowledged. For a time there would be little money with which to keep *The Haven* out of debt but he knew that one day he could do all that Adam had done for the poor people he had loved so much. Perhaps, Patrick thought, he and Sarah might even begin to instruct women in the skills of nursing – women who were gentle and compassionate; women like Sarah.

If only, he yearned, there could be some small hope that one day Sarah might come to care a little for him then he would walk proudly indeed in the mean streets, poor as a church-mouse though he may be.

It had pleased him that morning when Sarah seemed glad to see him, but surely it was only relief and gratitude that had made her eyes shine and her face take on a beauty that caused his breath to catch in his throat. She could not have felt as he felt; could not have known how he ached inside at the sight of her and the sound of her voice. It would not be easy for him to live at *The Haven*, so bittersweet to be near her yet so very far from her love.

He wanted her beside him now, knowing that just the nearness of her presence would be enough to set his pulses racing once more and his heart pounding with desperate longing.

If he willed it strongly enough, would she come to him? Would she come as she had come that first night with her hair loose about her shoulders?

Come to me, his heart yearned out to her. *Come to me again, my Sarah*.

And so it seemed that drawn by his intangible longing she came gently to his side and her footsteps were so soft that for a moment Patrick could only sense she was there.

For a little time they stood unspeaking, something in the magic around them forbidding almost that they should breathe.

Then Sarah said softly,

'I hoped I might find you here, Patrick.'

I wanted you to come, Patrick's heart exulted. *I called out to you with my love and you came!*

Sarah gazed ahead of her to where the first star hung low in the sky.

'There is something I must tell you, Patrick. I cannot keep it inside me any longer. There must be no secrets between us.'

It was inevitable that soon Patrick must find out that she owned *The Haven* and that he need have no fears for its security. But in telling him that, he would have to know too how high a price in human anguish it had cost. She would need to tell him that all she had known in her youth – the elegant establishment at which she had been educated, her clothes, the jewellery she had worn and the luxury into which she had been born was paid for by the misery of others – by the buying and selling of human life.

Then Patrick would learn she was Mad Jonathan Rigby's kin. Would he have the charity, she wondered, to believe that in her innocence she had known nothing of her grandfather's wickedness or indeed of his existence?

Patrick had once been very poor; it would likely give him satisfaction to know that in the end her grandfather's vast fortune had gone, she thought dully.

Sarah felt Patrick lay his hands gently on her shoulders, turning her to face him. He did not speak and Sarah drew courage from the familiar strength of his nearness.

'It would be unfair that you should not know, Patrick.'

He looked down at her troubled face and his heart contracted with pity. What could there be about Sarah that should cause her such anguish, he wondered. And whatever it was, did she imagine it could ever be so enormous as to make him stop loving her for one small second?

'Sarah,' he whispered gently, 'I do not know what it is that troubles you so and I do not care. To me you are Sarah and the dearest person I know. That is all that matters and all I care about.'

'But Patrick . . .'

'No, Sarah.'

He placed his forefinger tenderly on her lips for he was confident that there was only one thing he needed to know about her past life.

Once, he and Adam had talked about Sarah.

'*But have you made no enquiries about her background? She may be an erring wife who has run away . . .*'

Not that, he shuddered; anything at all but that.

But still he made himself ask the question of her.

'There is just one thing I want you to tell me, Sarah. I would not ask but it is important to me. All else doesn't matter.'

Even as the words tripped from his tongue, he cursed his stupidity. Why couldn't he let well alone?

'What is it?' Sarah whispered, her lips stiff.

'Are you a married woman, Sarah? Is there, somewhere, a man who has claim to you?'

Sarah's eyes jerked wide open.

'Married, Patrick?' She shook her head. 'Of course I am not married. Why should you think I was?'

Relief washed over Patrick. He heard his voice saying,

'I was certain you must be. What other reason could there have been to prevent you and Adam from marrying?'

'Adam and I? Marrying?'

She gave an embarrassed laugh.

'There was never any thoughts of marriage between us,' she said, incredulously.

'But you were lovers.'

He hated himself for what he was saying, but he had to know. 'I saw you in each other's arms, when Adam was ill. I wasn't spying, believe me Sarah; it was accidental –'

Sarah shook her head sadly.

'Adam and I were not lovers, Patrick. I loved him – I am proud to admit it – but the love I felt for Adam I would have felt for my brother had I had one or my mother, had I known her.'

She made a small, helpless gesture with her hands as though lost for words.

'You see, I loved Adam for what he tried to do. I respected him for his great compassion. If you saw us together in such a way I can only think I was trying to comfort him.'

'Oh, my dear, I have gone through unspeakable torment thinking you could never love me –'

'Love *you*, Patrick?'

'Yes, Sarah. Is it so very strange? I have loved you almost from the moment we met.'

'But I cannot believe it.'

She dropped her eyes, suddenly shy of him.

'I am Sarah – poor, plain Sarah. I have no dowry, Patrick; I am not beautiful.'

'You are beautiful to me!'

Triumphantly he reached out for her, cupping her face in his hands, forcing her eyes to meet his.

'You are the most beautiful thing in my life, Sarah. Can you understand what I have endured, loving you?'

'Forgive me, Patrick,' Sarah stammered. 'I didn't know.

Perhaps I should have, but I didn't. You were betrothed to Arabella and she was beautiful and rich and everything a man could want in a wife. I didn't so much as think you could ever have wanted me.'

'Everything I want is standing just the distance of a kiss away. She sat at my feet one night with her hair falling to her waist and from that moment on I loved her.'

Gently he removed the combs from the nape of her neck and her hair scattered about her in a gleaming fire-tinged fall, slipping and sliding like silk over his wrists.

'Now we are at the beginning, Sarah, with no misunderstandings or pledges to come between us. I shall teach you to love me!'

He buried his face in the red profusion of her hair and knew with a thrill of triumph that her body was trembling as crazily as his own.

'Now I can say what I wanted to say that first night we stood here together.'

Her body grew soft and yielding as he pulled her into his arms.

He wanted to tell her of his longing, of the fierce surging inside him that made every pulse in his body throb out a mad tattoo; he wanted to kiss her cheeks, her eyes, her lips; to tear down the stars and scatter them at her feet.

But his throat was tight and he could hardly breathe.

'I love you,' he whispered instead. 'I shall love you, Sarah Rigby, until the end of time.'

He felt her mouth near his. She was trying to speak his name but no sound came. Her lips, as they moved, felt like the brush of a butterfly's wing.

'Sarah,' he breathed as her arms stole round his neck. Then his mouth was on hers. It was just as he had known it would be and her body trembled with delight as he had so often dreamed it would.

'Oh, Sarah, my love, I want you so,' he whispered.

She did not reply but in the shyness of her eyes that mirrored the soft grey twilight, he saw the love for which he had been longing.

There was a star in the sky; bigger and brighter than all the rest, that seemed to glow above them, casting its light upon them like a benediction and suddenly Patrick knew with utter certainty that he would hear no more sighing. Now the gentle friend of his youth could rest beside the little Alms-houses with a peaceful soul.

'We will call our son Adam,' Patrick breathed as he looked with love at the star.

'The *first* of our sons,' Sarah whispered as her lips searched trembling again for his. 'The first of our sons, my darling.'